# GET THE GIRL

## Douglas I. Black

First published in 2016

# GET THE GIRL

DOUGLAS I. BLACK

*For Lucy and Josh*

# Chapter 1

*Butterfield Cottage, Rosie and Mark*

Mark burst through the front door of Butterfield Cottage with his phone clamped to his ear and a scowl on his face. He stopped a short distance into the cavernous hallway and stood stock-still with his legs wide apart and his free hand on his hip. While he listened intently to the voice on the phone, his wife, Rosie, appeared at the doorway and then tiptoed silently around him towards Jilly and I. She was followed by a uniformed man who, I assumed, was their chauffeur, struggling to carry a matching set of Louis Vuitton suitcases and travel bags.

Mark didn't move an inch as they squeezed past him, until the chauffeur, unable to continue his balancing act, dropped one of the bags. Mark turned and snarled at the unfortunate man while raising the palm of his hand so that it was only a few inches from his face. The man recoiled and then moved quickly away from Mark while Rosie retrieved the bag lying at his feet. When Rosie and the chauffeur reached Jilly and I, we helped them to place the bags noiselessly on the tiled floor. We all stood silently while Mark, the palm of his hand now raised in our direction, continued to listen to the voice on his phone. Without making a sound, Jilly and Rosie embraced and then I leant forward and kissed Rosie.

Suddenly, Mark erupted into life, bellowing, "Stop, stop, stop! I've heard enough, Paul. You're beginning to irritate me."

There was a pause while Mark, head down, began pacing around the hallway. Despite the fact that I was a bit pissed off at having to wait until Mark was good and ready to say hello, I couldn't help but admire the tall, blond and athletic figure that stood before me. Maybe it was his beautifully tailored Savile Row chalk stripe suit or his full head of lustrous hair but, in his mid-forties, he looked the epitome of health and style. My train of thought was interrupted as Mark began to shout again.

"Yes, of course I'm still here. Let me think!" And then after another lengthy pause, "Fuck'em. If the CEO doesn't know the unit cost or how much capital they need to break even, then I'm not interested. I'm even less interested now that you tell me that they are ruling out any sort of future M&A transaction in favour of an IPO."

Mark then abruptly ended his, to me at least, indecipherable conversation, turned to Jilly and I and beamed a huge smile.

"Jilly, darling, how are you?" he drawled, "You look absolutely gorgeous."

He kissed her on both cheeks before turning to me and saying, "Hello Tom, you lard-arse, you look like shit. You've been at the biscuit tin again haven't you?"

We hugged each other before Mark turned to the chauffeur and began barking instructions at him. "Leave the laptop here and take the other bags up to the Wellington Suite. It's the third room on the right on the second floor." He turned to us again, "Apparently the Wellington Suite has the best internet reception so I'm afraid I'm going to have to claim it for Rosie and I. I will be working on a document this weekend and I need access to the web."

I could see out of the corner of my eye that Jilly was not best pleased with Mark's presumption that his requirements came above all other considerations. She didn't say anything, but I noticed her rapidly blinking which was a sure sign that she was upset or angry. Thankfully, we had put our bags in the Nelson Suite; otherwise Jilly would almost certainly have said something. I was relieved that the weekend hadn't got off to a tense start. I could tell that Rosie, who had blushed slightly when Mark had announced which room he had chosen, was as happy as I was that there was to be no confrontation over the sleeping arrangements.

Jilly and I had arrived at Butterfield Cottage, as planned, at 4 p.m. and my first thought was that 'Cottage' didn't really do the place justice. I shouldn't have been surprised, I suppose, because I had left the arrangements to Mark and he had not stayed anywhere that wasn't the ultimate in luxury for more than fifteen years. Butterfield Cottage was, in fact, a six bedroomed, beautifully renovated 17th Century manor house set in twenty acres of parkland in the middle of Wiltshire. It boasted a tennis court, an indoor swimming pool and fabulous formal gardens. There were stables, a paddock, a walled vegetable garden, ancient orchards and a series of man-made lakes. Mark had persuaded me that we had all been working "terribly hard" and that we should get out of London for the weekend and have a well deserved autumn break in the country. He had told me that he would sort something out and that it was his treat. I wasn't comfortable with him paying, so I insisted that we share the cost. I sent him the cheque for five hundred pounds for my 'half' and he did the rest, or more accurately, his secretary did the rest.

Of course, he had lied about the cost, which would have been many thousands of pounds for the three nights we were staying. We had a cook, cleaners that came every morning and a couple of gamekeepers who would take us fishing or shooting if we wanted. The truth was that Jilly and I couldn't really afford our 'half' share. We had school fees to pay for our sons for another few years, a huge mortgage on a house that, according to the newspapers had recently lost twenty percent of its value, large credit card balances and outstanding loans on both our cars. By most standards we were well-off, but life seemed to be an unending financial struggle. I couldn't seem to get ahead and I couldn't see my way out. I was forty-six years old, doing a job I didn't like, with seemingly no chance of escape for at least ten years. To make things worse, the company I worked for had just announced that it was going to make ten percent of its workforce redundant. Like a lot of other organisations, Glenderma, an IT company, had fared badly in the recession that had started over a year previously and still seemed to be in full swing in October 2009. The rumour was that the job cuts would mostly be made to middle management and I was firmly in that category. My wife, Jilly, on the other hand, was secure in her senior management job and felt no sense of being trapped. She was the main earner in our family and loved jetting off around the world to a series of meetings and conferences.

Mark and Rosie arrived at 10 p.m. on that Friday evening and had, rather predictably, travelled in style. Their original intention was to drive down from London after lunch, but Mark had got dragged in on, what he described as, a "leveraged buyout acquisition debt problem." I had no idea what he meant by this, but I did know that as a partner in Emerson Venture Capital he had made many millions of pounds over the last fifteen years or so. In the end, Mark and Rosie had got a helicopter from somewhere in London to a private airport nearby and then rented a Range Rover for the final leg of the journey to Butterfield Cottage.

—

I had first met Rosie more than twenty-five years earlier. It was the beginning of the Easter holidays in 1981, just before my A Levels, and two friends and myself had gone to stay for a week with Patrick, another friend from school. We had all just turned eighteen and were looking forward to a few days of mayhem in Cornwall. Our plan was to get drunk, go bodyboarding, get high on magic mushrooms and get laid. As it turned out, we managed to achieve our first three objectives but tried and failed to achieve our fourth, and most important goal. Rosie was the fifteen year-old younger sister of Patrick. She was a slight, shy and quiet girl who hung around with us for most of the week. The others didn't seem to notice her at all and I couldn't understand it. I thought she was beautiful. She was average height, willowy, with long, fine, dark-brown hair to the middle of her back and her skin was pale, almost translucent. I was smitten with her from the moment I saw her, but because she was Patrick's younger sister and three years younger than me, I couldn't show it, never mind act upon it.

In the evenings, Rosie's parents allowed her to hang around with us until 10 p.m., after which, she had to go home. The stories that we told when we got back to school were all about getting drunk, the girls we nearly 'shagged' at the local discos and 'streaking' on the beach, but the highlight of my week was sitting outside the pub between 7 and 10 p.m. every evening when Rosie was there. I didn't even talk to her much. I just larked around with the others listening to songs from *Squeeze*, *The Specials* and *Adam and the Ants* wafting through the windows of the pub. We drank beer, smoked, shared the odd spliff and jumped about a bit. The longest conversation I had with Rosie was about *Adam and the Ants*. I teased her about fancying Adam and told her that he had "sold out" and hadn't made a good record since 1979. I acted cool, or tried to, but really I was jealous of her fancying Adam and longed to kiss her.

One evening at the pub particularly stuck in my mind. Earlier that day, my three friends and I had decided to dye our hair blond like the band members of *The Police*. We had used lemon juice and cheap dye from the chemist and it hadn't really worked. I had only used lemon juice which, unsurprisingly, didn't work at all. The others had used the dye and their hair now had a green tinge. I was wearing a stripy T-shirt, just like Sting's, and jeans. I thought I looked great. At some point that evening, Rosie and I found ourselves sitting next to each other on the low wall outside the pub. The truth was that I had worked out an elaborate plan to sit casually next to her without giving myself away to my friends as having the slightest interest in her. As we sat there, our bare arms touched and that was enough for me to, for a short while, lose all ability to speak. When I regained the power of speech, I asked Rosie for a cigarette. She had just lit up and she passed her cigarette to me. I took a drag and realised that the butt was still damp from her mouth. It was like having an electric shock pass through my body.

Just over a year later in the summer of 1982, a group of us had gone down to Cornwall again, and this time Mark was with us. I had been trying to get Patrick to invite me back down to Cornwall ever since that first Easter trip. Despite my lack of conversations with Rosie, I'd had real difficulty getting her out of my head and was desperate to see her again. Part of me was hoping that, with a year of university and a little more experience with girls under my belt, the seventeen year old Rosie would have less of a disarming impact on me. The bigger part of me couldn't wait to see her again and

I was curious as to how much she had changed over the last couple of years. In fact, she looked very similar. Her pale skin was still beautifully unblemished, her long, dark hair was the same length and her slender figure was unchanged. I acted as cool as I could around her while trying to make the right impression by being friendly and funny. She, in return, was genial and relaxed without giving any real indication that she was attracted to me in the same way as I was definitely still attracted to her.

Mark made it quite obvious from his first meeting with Rosie that he was very interested in her. To my horror, she seemed to welcome his interest and coyly flirted with him at every opportunity. I tried not to show it and I think I succeeded, but the fact that they seemed to be getting on so well made me feel physically ill. I couldn't concentrate properly on anything. I couldn't relax and, at times, when I was in her company, I simply couldn't string a coherent sentence together. I had been so looking forward to seeing Rosie again and had naively imagined that the extra worldliness that I had gained since I'd last seen her would mean that she would be mine. But I was being so... so naive. Horrifyingly, she seemed to have fallen for the charms of Mark. I shouldn't have been surprised. Of course Mark would get the girl.

Mark and I had first met in 1976 at the age of thirteen when we arrived as 'new boys' for our first term at St. Michael's College. This Roman Catholic boarding school, run by priests, was the place that we were going to spend the next five years of our lives. Most of the 'new boys' had arrived from one of two feeder schools so it meant that Mark and I, who hadn't, were very much the outsiders.

My bond with Mark was formed on our first night at St Michael's when we were beaten for talking after 'lights out'. There was no gentle settling in to the school or allowances made for boys who were spending their first night away from home. We were warned once by our housemaster, Father Matthew. Then, when we were caught talking a second time, told to get up and follow him to his study. As we stood there, shivering in our pyjamas, I don't think either of us expected what happened next. Father Matthew marched to a cupboard in the corner of his study, found a suitably whippy cane, and proceeded to give us six of the best. The thin cotton of our pyjamas offered little protection and the weals across our backsides remained with us for a couple of weeks. There was pain and shock but no resentment. What we both managed to do was avoid crying or making any sound at all while we were being beaten. We had immediate respect for each other and over the next few weeks, as we saw many of our peers cry uncontrollably when caned, this respect and friendship grew.

It was through sport, particularly rugby, that Mark and I moved quickly from being 'outsiders' to being accepted as fully integrated members of the school. Initially it was me that made the bigger impact on the rugby field. I had matured early and was unusually strong and tall for a boy who had just arrived at St. Michael's. It was obvious, from the first training session, that I would be in the 'A' team. Mark, on the other hand, was still physically a young boy and he had to rely more on skill than strength. It was much less clear-cut whether he would join me in the top team, but in the end he just scraped in. That was the last time that I had the upper hand over Mark.

After his brief brush with mediocrity, Mark then excelled at everything else he did in his first year at St Michael's. He was outstanding at all the other sports, none of which were as dependent as rugby upon size and strength. He played an active role in the drama and debating clubs and he was academically exceptional. Most importantly, in terms of his popularity with the other boys, he did all of this without seeming to try too hard. From time to time Mark would find himself in trouble with the school authorities. The trouble he got himself into was never particularly serious, but it did mean he got caned occasionally and that meant his credibility with his fellow pupils was further enhanced.

As we progressed through the school, the gap between Mark's achievements and mine grew larger. By the beginning of our second year my physical advantage over him on the rugby field had disappeared. He had shot up in height over the summer and he was nearly as tall as me when we returned to school. He was no longer scraping into the rugby team and he was made captain of both the hockey and cricket teams for our year. In fact, halfway through the summer term of our second year at St Michael's, he was selected for the school 1st XI at cricket. All of a sudden he wasn't just a sporting star in our year, he began to be known and respected by the older boys at St. Michael's.

Mark's higher profile also brought him to the attention of the girls at the school. Although St. Michael's was a traditional boys' boarding school, in the sixth form, girls from a local convent school joined the boys. These seventeen and eighteen year old girls seemed incredibly glamorous to the boys in the lower years at St. Michael's. We regarded them in the same way that we regarded female film or pop stars. To us they were sexy, gorgeous and, most of all, completely unobtainable. Rather incredibly, shortly after Mark had got into the Cricket 1st XI, one of these beautiful creatures actually spoke to him. She stopped him in the corridor to congratulate him. She even knew his name.

Mark's 'hero' status was enhanced even further during the next year. This was partly because he was excelling academically and had managed to get into the top teams at the school for all major sports. However, it was mainly because, while still in the fifth form and only sixteen years old, he started going out with Lizzy Yates, the best looking girl in the Upper Sixth. This was unheard of and confirmed him as the 'golden boy' of the school. Mark took all of this success in his stride and, for the most part, remained unaffected by it. There were no signs at that time of any arrogance and the two of us remained the best of friends. Our final two years at St. Michael's carried on in much the same vein as our first three. Tall, blond and 'golden', Mark continued to have great success in everything he did. His success on the sports field and with the opposite sex continued, unabated, and when he won a place at Oxford University no one was particularly surprised. As his shorter, darker and stockier best mate, I was a little bit overshadowed by him. But none of this got in the way of our friendship and we left St. Michael's determined that, whatever life held in store for us, we would always be best mates.

# Chapter 2

## *Friday at Butterfield Cottage*

Mark called me early that Friday evening, just after Jilly and I had arrived at the Cottage, to tell me that I should instruct the cook to prepare supper for about 10.30 p.m. It was typical of him to neither consider whether the cook would still be on duty that late in the evening, or whether Jilly and I would prefer to eat at a more normal time. No, for Mark, there was only one person who needed to be considered and that was him. It wasn't really that he thought his requirements should take precedence; it was more that he didn't even begin the process of thinking about anyone but himself. This attitude not only applied to his friends but also extended to Rosie and his two young sons.

Rosie and Mark had been married for just over twelve years. He had finally proposed to her, confiding in me that "thirty-four is a perfect age for a man like me to marry." I am sure he loved Rosie as much as he was capable of loving anyone when he proposed, it was just that he was incapable of truly loving anyone but himself. Rosie had been chosen, he explained, because she was exactly "the sort of girl that a man like me should marry. She's a couple of years younger than me, she's beautiful, from a good family and hasn't been around the block too many times." Rosie, on the other hand, had never loved anyone but Mark. It had infuriated me when she had, predictably, fallen for him all those years ago in Cornwall. He had broken her heart on several occasions between then and when he finally married her, but Mark always seemed to have a hold on Rosie. He also seemed to have the same hold on their two sons for whom his love seemed anything but unconditional. Mark was only really loving when his two young boys were succeeding outrageously. For his younger son, Hamish, who was a clone of Mark, this was easy. He was regularly top of his class academically and seemed to be captain of every sports team he played for. For his elder son, Tim, life was much more of a battle. It was heartbreaking to see him so desperate for his father's approval but never quite being able to gain it. Mark didn't so much criticise him as ignore him.

Mark was in a foul mood when he arrived. This put everyone else on edge. He often had this effect on people. To those he wanted to impress he was charm itself, but for those less crucial to his ambitions he could be, and often was, overbearing and endlessly demanding. He was also quite often rude and insulting to Rosie in public. This particularly annoyed me, as it struck me as totally unnecessary. If Rosie had been feisty and confrontational, this behaviour could have been seen as just a bit of public sparring, but this was not the case. Rosie was gentle, non confrontational and would never say anything in public that would embarrass Mark. He behaved this way because he knew he could get away with it.

Following their arrival, once Mark had finished shouting at, a probably cowering, Paul on the other end of the phone line, he banged on for a good half an hour about the latest happenings at his business and how "fucking incompetent" everyone was. When he finally finished, he asked me how things were for me. I couldn't really think of anything to say other than, "Same as," but I tried to sound enthusiastic about the latest developments at Glenderma Solutions. I might have managed it, had Mark not interrupted me before I had even completed my first sentence to announce that we better go through to supper or we'd be taking advantage of the staff. As if he cared. We wandered through the house until we eventually found the dining room. It was quite an extraordinary place. The Georgian dining table, while only set for the four of us, could comfortably have seated twenty. There were original paintings on the walls and, most incredible of all, a couple of waitresses waiting to dance attendance on us. The food was a delicious fusion of French and English country cuisine. Foie gras was followed by turbot and then pheasant, which, in turn, were followed by a huge selection of cheeses and a choice of three desserts. I wished that Jilly and I hadn't been so hungry an hour or so earlier and had a snack of beans on toast.

Over dinner, Mark regaled us with a list of the celebrities he'd recently met. They ranged from junior ministers in the Labour Government, through actors to sportsmen. Mark's particular favourite were professional cricketers. I love cricket, but I was always surprised by Mark's apparently insatiable desire to meet and befriend famous ex-cricketers. He announced that, as a treat for

Rosie, he had invited three former players and their wives to join us the next day for a range of activities. They would also be joining us for dinner the next evening and staying the night. I could tell that Rosie was less than ecstatic. She had absolutely no interest in cricket and had told me earlier, when Mark was on the phone, that she was really looking forward to a quiet weekend with just old friends. She also mentioned that she had hardly seen Mark over the last few months due to his endless work, cricket and charity commitments. Mark was one of those people who needed to be endlessly busy.

Rosie could have laughed and questioned Mark as to how he could possibly think that meeting ex-cricketers could be considered a treat for her, but she didn't. Long experience had taught her that any questioning, let alone challenging, of Mark would just lead to a barrage of insults and accusations of ingratitude. She duly thanked Mark for his thoughtfulness while Jilly and I suppressed our laughter. I was a bit miffed to find out that, while I would be joining Mark and the three male guests for fly-fishing the next morning, I wouldn't be able to go quad biking with them in the afternoon due to the lack of a fifth bike. In fact, I was more than a bit miffed. While I had no particular desire to spend my time with three guys that I didn't know, I was deeply pissed off at being treated like a second-class citizen. My only consolation was that I had, long ago, realised that there was only one first class citizen in Mark's life.

Mark had not always been like this. Since the beginning of our friendship at school, and all through our twenties we had remained incredibly close. Mark always had a fierce determination to succeed, but I, and everyone else in our group of friends, still thought of him as easy-going, loyal and great fun to be with. During our thirties we hadn't spent as much time together because of various family and work commitments, but he seemed pretty unchanged to me. We always had a great time in each other's company and Mark was well liked and regarded by everybody I knew.

At some point in his late thirties, this began to change. Maybe it was the fact that he had become increasingly successful. Perhaps you get used to 'calling the shots' and people doing exactly what you say. Perhaps power really does corrupt. Or perhaps it was just a function of age. Whatever it was, Mark had changed and the rate of change had accelerated markedly in the last few years. We still had fun from time to time, but mostly I was left wondering what had happened to my old friend. The change in his behaviour towards Rosie was the thing that really angered me. Besides being beautiful, Rosie was gentle and very easy-going. Mark, increasingly, just ran roughshod over her. He took all the family decisions without even consulting her. He rarely asked her to attend his business or social functions and, generally, just treated her as if she was his personal assistant or housekeeper. What was really unpalatable to me was that, apart from when he wanted to impress a business contact or a cricketer that he was sucking up to, he would belittle her in public or just completely ignore her. In short, he was cruel and abusive to Rosie and that, I found difficult to stomach.

# Chapter 3

## *Jilly*

My wife, Jilly, and I first came across each other at Coventry University. She was studying History and I was reading Economics. While our paths did not cross in the lecture theatre, as new arrivals we were at all the same events during 'Freshers' Week' and at lots of the same parties during our first year at university. I noticed her almost immediately. She was tall, slim and athletic looking. Her natural blonde hair framed a pretty, even-featured face, and she exuded an easy confidence. She attracted an awful lot of attention, both from her fellow first years and from the second and third year men who had arrived back at university a week early in order to 'check-out' the new 'talent' at Freshers' Week.

I joined both the Federation of Conservative Students and the Folk Club purely because Jilly had. I had no interest in either politics or folk music, but it seemed a good idea if I was to have a chance of getting to know her better. The ultimate aim was to 'pull' Jilly, but, to be honest, I didn't really think I had much of a chance. I wasn't a bad looking chap, but in terms of 'pulling' the good looking girls there always seemed to be quite a few better looking or more confident boys ahead of me in the queue. Sure enough, by the time Freshers' Week was over, Jilly was seeing a second year student. He was tall, good-looking and confident and my, perhaps unrealistic, hopes had been dashed. I wasn't too disappointed because, although I wasn't without my charms, deep down I had always expected a 'Mark type' to get there first.

I struggled during that first term at university. Although I had been at a boarding school for five years I was incredibly homesick. In fact homesick was the wrong word, I didn't miss home at all, I missed St Michael's. At university no one cared that you had been a member of the Rugby 1st XV, that you had been a prefect or that you had been part of the 'cool crowd'. The close friendships I had formed with my schoolmates, many of which would last a lifetime, were irrelevant. I was thrown together with a boy whom I had never met, but whose surname was next in the alphabet to mine. We shared bunk beds in a tiny room in our halls of residence, went to all the same lectures and socialised together. I spent twenty-four hours a day with Colin Billings for my first thirteen weeks at university.

Colin was short, overweight and had disgusting personal habits. His father was a lifelong City financier and two years previously, when Colin was sixteen, he had left London to take up a post in Singapore. Colin had spent the last two summers there with him, but for the rest of the time he had been left very much to his own devices. He had spent the Christmas and Easter holidays staying at various relatives' or friends' houses. He had no base in England and, as a result had, by the time he arrived at university, become very self-reliant.

This self-reliance did not however extend to being able or willing to wash any of his clothes. Obviously when he first arrived at university his clothes were clean, but after a month or so they were either soiled, smelly or both. Every morning he would go through a process of smelling his underwear to see which of his pants and socks were the least offensive. He would then cheerfully don these soiled undergarments, pull on a pair of jeans, a T-shirt and a jumper, and saunter off to lectures. We would walk together to our lectures and apart from the vague smell of stale sweat which surrounded him, Colin would also stop occasionally to heave up some phlegm from his throat and spit into the gutter. Strangely, I quite liked Colin, but sometimes, when he behaved like a pig in the confines of our shared bedroom, it was all I could do to stop myself from punching him.

Colin was popular despite his habits. He was always lively, upbeat and amusing and I suppose this was why both men and women were keen to be in his company. This proved very useful when it came to Jilly. She was always surrounded by at least a couple of her girlfriends, which made it difficult, at least in my mind, to approach her. Colin had no such problem and at one of the parties during our first term, he struck up a conversation with her. She seemed hugely amused by whatever he was saying and didn't seem put off by, what I had now come to regard as, Colin's 'stench'.

Through Colin, I became increasingly friendly with Jilly. When he started going out with one of her friends, I was convinced that Jilly and I would get together, despite the fact that she already had a boyfriend. There was a group of about eight of us that hung around together a lot. It was the usual mix of house parties, university society functions and just generally socialising in pubs and the Student's Union. There were quite a few drunken gropes and snogs going on in our group, but although Jilly was extremely flirty and tactile with me, she remained completely faithful to her boyfriend during that first year at university.

It was probably obvious to Jilly that all I really wanted was to be with her. However, for the most part she treated me as if I was a naughty schoolboy who wasn't in her 'league' and therefore, romantically, wasn't worthy of consideration. I tried to make Jilly jealous by 'getting off' with girls in front of her or by lavishing attention on her girlfriends, but nothing seemed to work. She, on the other hand, was able to raise my hopes in a variety of different ways. She would laugh at my jokes, or snuggle up to me on a sofa, or brush past me in a way that I thought must be deliberate, but nothing ever happened between us.

Towards the end of our first year, my hopes were further raised when Jilly finished with her boyfriend. I talked to Jilly in the aftermath of her first university relationship, hoping that she would see me as sensitive and a bit more grown up than she had previously thought. I was hoping that the break up, although her choice, would leave her vulnerable and a bit upset. The truth was that, although her former boyfriend was distraught to have lost the 'love of his life', she was pretty much unaffected. She didn't need consoling or looking after as I had hoped, she was looking forward to "being single for a while." Jilly was not just lusted over by me, but an awful lot of others. She had quite a few casual relationships during our second year at university and left a string of broken hearts in her wake. She didn't appear to understand the effect she was having on these potential suitors. One guy that she dated for a couple of weeks – on what she considered a casual basis, but he considered deadly serious – spent six weeks crying every time he had a drink once she had ended their relationship. Bearing in mind that he drank most days to alleviate his pain, he did an awful lot of weeping.

However, everything changed during the summer term of my second year at Coventry. I was living in a house-share with Colin and some other students. Patrick, my old friend from school, came to stay with me for the weekend. I met him at the railway station and to my complete surprise he turned up with his sister, Rosie. She had just been 'chucked' again by Mark and was very upset and even more beautiful than when I last saw her. I was absolutely delighted that Rosie was there. Mark had been going out with her, on and off, for nearly a year. They had got together shortly after their first meeting in Cornwall. He had then finished with her at the end of the Christmas holidays of his second year. He explained to me that her visits to Oxford were making his life difficult in terms of other romantic interests he had at university. Mark then persuaded Rosie the following Easter to resume their relationship before finishing with her, once again, when things got a bit complicated.

After getting over the initial surprise of seeing her arrive with Patrick, I set about convincing Rosie that I would make a much better boyfriend than Mark. I casually let her know that while I'd had a couple of relationships over the last two years, none of them were particularly serious, and that I was currently single. I sat next to her all night, cracking jokes and giving her consoling hugs to cheer her up. She told me that she hadn't laughed for two weeks and that it was lovely to see me again. While I was encouraged by her reaction to me, I decided that now was not the right time for me to make a move and that it was better to wait until she made the first approach. It occurred to me that, in the two years that I'd known her, there had never seemed to be a good time to make a move. She'd either been 'too young' or going out with Mark or getting over Mark. I thought that maybe there was never going to be a perfect time and that maybe I should just go for it, but in the end I didn't. I contented myself with the notion that patience would win the day and that, in the meantime, I would just enjoy being in her company.

Everyone seemed to like Patrick and Rosie. At first, Jilly did her normal thing of flirting with the new man that had joined our group. It was as if she needed to reassure herself that every man she met fancied her, just so that she could make it clear to them that she was out of their league. I could see this pattern of behaviour unfolding in front of me just as it had done so many times before. I could see that Patrick thought he had made quite an impact on her. It was at this point that

Jilly would become gradually less flirtatious and less interested. On this occasion, however, the change wasn't gradual, it was very sudden. Jilly stopped flirting with Patrick and became very flirty with me. She sat next to me, draped herself over me, laughed at my jokes and nuzzled into my neck. I would like to say that I made the most of the situation, but I didn't. There I was, sitting in between the only two girls that I had ever loved, both of whom were all over me – well, perhaps Rosie wasn't all over me, but she was certainly enjoying my company - and I panicked. It was too much for me. I got up and joined Patrick at the bar and pretended that Jilly hadn't been flirting outrageously with me, or I would have done if Patrick had allowed me to. He immediately announced that Jilly was a "prick–teasing bitch" and that he couldn't believe that she fancied me not him. I reassured him that she definitely didn't fancy me and that she was just having fun.

We stayed at the pub for another couple of hours before heading home. I've got to say that I went home feeling pretty good. Jilly had continued to lavish attention on me, while Rosie had laughed at my jokes and cuddled me affectionately. When Jilly left with her housemates she gave me a long, lingering kiss on the lips and pressed herself up against me. Patrick said he didn't like her and Rosie teased me about my new "girlfriend." I walked home in a state of elation, with one arm around Patrick and the other around Rosie.

Patrick slept in my room with me, while Rosie slept in an absent flatmate's bedroom. I woke in the late morning and immediately began thinking about the events of the night before. What did Jilly's long, lingering kiss mean? Was Rosie just being affectionate to an old friend or did she feel something for me? Which of these two girls, both of whom I had previously thought to be unobtainable, did I prefer? I got out of bed and went to make some tea. I made three cups, one each for Rosie, Patrick and myself. Patrick was a bit confused when I brought his tea to him. He opened one eye, farted and told me to "fuck off and let me sleep". I didn't care because I had only gone to the trouble of making tea so that I would have the excuse of seeing Rosie as soon as possible.

I knocked softly on her door and quietly entered the room. Lying on her side, Rosie did not stir and I took a moment to stare at her perfect face. Rosie's dark brown hair was spread across the pillow as if it had been specially arranged. Her hands were placed together, as if in prayer, under her perfect face with its unblemished skin. It had been an unusually warm night and she had discarded the duvet in favour of a sheet. I could see the outline of her slight frame under the sheet and I remember thinking that I'd never seen anything so beautiful. I moved towards the bed and nudged her very gently on the shoulder. She immediately stirred and opened her eyes. Her look of surprise was almost immediately replaced by a big smile. At that moment I knew, although I fancied Jilly and lusted after her, that the delicate and sweet girl in front of me was the one that I really wanted.

Unfortunately, Rosie immediately broke the spell. She kissed me on the cheek, thanked me for the tea and said that I was the most thoughtful person she knew. She went on to say that I was the big brother she wished she'd had rather than Patrick. I smiled at her to hide the fact that I was crushed and left the room without saying a word because I feared that, if I opened my mouth, I would say something that I regretted.

The bedroom Rosie was staying in was on the ground floor and, as I left the room, I turned to my right to see Colin opening the front door to Jilly. There I was, in my boxer shorts and T-shirt, coming out of Rosie's bedroom. Colin and Jilly came to the obvious conclusion and followed me into the kitchen teasing me about having 'slept' with Rosie. Neither of them had any idea how much I wished they had been right and that, to Rosie, I was something more than someone who she loved like a brother. Even through my pain I noticed that while Colin was taking the piss in a completely normal way, Jilly's tone was a bit more aggressive. She called me a cradle snatcher and inferred that Rosie was a bit of a tart as she hadn't wasted any time, having just finished with Mark, before moving onto the next bloke. This angered me and I immediately leapt to Rosie's defence. For the first time since I had known Jilly, I shouted at her. I told her to shut up and never to speak about Rosie in that way again. I was just about to ask her what she was doing at our flat at this time in the morning when she burst into tears and ran out of the front door.

I was completely confused. Jilly had never shown that kind of emotion in all the time that I'd known her. She had always seemed so in control. I had never seen her upset. Colin explained the situation to me with the subtlety that only a man who thought that personal hygiene meant smelling slightly better than a tramp, could. He said that it was obvious to everyone that I fancied Rosie like mad, and that because, for once, I hadn't been following Jilly around like a lapdog, she'd become jealous. At least he didn't spit into the sink while he gave me lessons in love.

I kept things light and friendly with Rosie until she and Patrick left later that weekend. She appeared to have no idea how I felt, how much I struggled to be near her when I knew she was not interested in me in the same way I was in her. Every time she sat next to me in a pub or at the table, I found it difficult to concentrate. When she draped her bare legs over mine on the sofa while we watched television, I was in my own personal purgatory. The porcelain silkiness of her skin next to mine was heavenly, but it was hell knowing that, to her, I was just a "really good friend."

On Sunday evening, after Patrick and Rosie had departed, I went to see Jilly. She was alone in her house and answered the door in her pyjamas. She looked like she had been crying. I was taken by surprise by how vulnerable and small she looked. I had always thought of Jilly as this tall, athletic girl for whom life was easy. She was comfortable and confident with her Amazonian looks and always seemed to be terribly sure of herself. She revelled in the fact that virtually every man at university would have jumped at the chance to be in her company, never mind go out with her. This was not the same girl that stood in front of me on that sultry spring evening.

Jilly invited me inside and offered me a cup of coffee. As we entered the kitchen, I noticed that she had no makeup on and I remember thinking that she looked quite different from her normal self. She was no less good-looking, she just looked different. I apologised for shouting at her the previous morning, but explained that Rosie really didn't deserve to be spoken about in that way. So, it was an apology – but a qualified one. I was determined that she should, if not apologise for what she had said, then at least recognise that she had got Rosie all wrong. Jilly did neither. She walked towards me, kissed me on the lips and, without saying a word, took me by the hand and led me upstairs to her bedroom.

Her bedroom was nothing like mine. It was warm, comfortable and clean. It had a desk with neatly labelled files stacked on top of it, a dressing table, a wardrobe and proper curtains. In my nervousness I started to compliment her on the décor. Jilly put her finger on my lips and stopped me mid sentence. She took a couple of steps backwards, looked straight at me, unbuttoned her pyjama top and dropped it to the floor. While maintaining her gaze, she then stepped out of her pyjama bottoms and stood completely naked in front of me. Her legs were slightly apart and she suddenly looked completely confident. I stood motionless and speechless. She was perfect. Maybe it was the light in her bedroom, but her skin gave off a golden glow. She had high, full breasts, a tiny waist and beautiful, curved hips. I had imagined Jilly naked on many occasions, but the reality was almost overwhelming. She stepped forward put her arms around my waist, gently pulled me towards her and looked up at me. We stared at each other for what seemed like an eternity and then she gently kissed me. I couldn't believe what was happening, but before I could say anything her hand reached behind my head and pulled me more firmly onto her now open mouth.

The next week or so passed in a haze. Jilly and I spent every moment together, mostly in bed. I had never been happier, never had fewer worries and I couldn't quite believe my luck. What was even more unbelievable was that this perfect girl seemed to be just as ecstatic as I was. Jilly was naked almost all of the time and I never quite got used to the sight of her fantastic body or the fact that she seemed as besotted with me as I was with her. When we eventually decided that we should perhaps return to lectures, I knew that life would never be the same for me again.

# Chapter 4

## *Saturday at Butterfield Cottage*

Mark gave the instruction to Jilly, Rosie and myself during dinner on Friday evening that we needed to be at breakfast by 8 a.m. the next morning. This was so that we would be ready for the gamekeepers' arrival at 9 a.m. and the arrival of his guests at 9.30 a.m. I didn't drink much during dinner, maybe a bottle or so of red, so that I would be fresh for the next day's activities. Unfortunately, I had a restless night, waking at 2 a.m. and then again at 5 a.m. before getting back to sleep. Consequently when the alarm went off at 7.30 a.m. I was absolutely exhausted. Since the age of about forty I had found that alcohol increasingly had this effect on me. I could get off to sleep easily enough, but I would, invariably, have a restless night and feel pretty grim the next morning.

Having dragged myself out of bed, Jilly and I were at the breakfast table at 8 a.m. on the dot. Butterfield Cottage was, according to the brochure, famous for its breakfasts and there was the most amazing spread laid out on the side-tables around the room. It was a bit pathetic really, but I was excited about the huge range of food. It initially reminded me of the breakfasts served at one of the famous, five star London hotels, but actually on closer inspection, this was much better than that. It was the sort of breakfast that I had seen in various films depicting life in an Edwardian country house. A fruit course opened the proceedings. Pink, green and yellow melons cut into slices, baskets of apples and peaches with grapes hanging over the rim and plates of pears. This was followed by hors d'oeuvres and then the cooked food. This included lamb, veal chops, bacon or ham. These were served with a selection of either a salad of sliced tomatoes or poached (boiled, if you preferred) eggs on toast or omelette. Alternatively you could have fish, (broiled or sautéed), devilled lobster or something called steamed finnan haddie. This was all followed, rather incredibly, by a dessert of frozen punch, pastry or jellies. Hot muffins or waffles and syrup were also available with coffee.

My excitement at the breakfast spread was soured by a change in mood when Rosie joined us. She informed us that Mark wouldn't be down until about 10 a.m. He had received a text from his guests and they wouldn't be able to make it until 11 a.m. I asked Rosie when Mark had got the text, thinking that his guests had been quite rude to not let us know earlier. It was quite difficult to get the information out of Rosie, but it transpired that they had texted Mark the previous evening. Rather typically, Mark just hadn't bothered to tell anyone.

I was determined not to let the situation get to me. After all, we had a great breakfast to enjoy and I was already feeling better after my restless night. After we had eaten, I went outside to chat to the gamekeepers who had arrived in their Landrovers at 9 a.m. as planned. I explained that we wouldn't be setting off for our fly-fishing expedition until late morning, as our guests had been unavoidably delayed. They seemed quite relaxed about the situation and said that there were always things to do on the estate so they would busy themselves for a couple of hours. They were probably used to the fact that the sort of people who could afford a weekend at Butterfield Cottage, were also the sort of people who suited themselves and kept others waiting.

Mark's guests duly arrived at 11 a.m. with their wives in tow. Mark had sauntered down to breakfast half an hour earlier and complained that there was "no fucker about and the food's cold." He eventually satisfied himself with a cup of coffee and a bacon sandwich. On greeting his guests however, Mark's demeanour changed from po-faced and chippy to bright and sparky in an instant. This was the Mark that I knew of old. He was enthusiastic, polite and charming. He shook hands heartily with the men and flashed a winning smile at each of their wives before kissing them on both cheeks. Mark then turned to the gamekeepers and asked them to take the new arrivals' luggage up to their rooms. I could tell from their reaction that they were a bit taken aback by Mark's request. They had probably never been asked to take on the role of porters before, but Mark made his request with such authority that they just shrugged their shoulders and did as they were told.

Two Landrovers took our party of ten up to Loscombe Lake, which was situated at the far end of the estate and had recently been stocked with large numbers of brown trout. I had only been fishing a couple of times before and was not that enthusiastic about the prospect, but what a great time we had. Mark had somehow found time in between his business, charity and sporting commitments to become a bit of an expert. He knew exactly which fly to use and cast his rod with effortless grace. He also showed huge patience while schooling his guests in the finer arts of fly-fishing. Jilly, Rosie and I had the full attention of the gamekeepers who provided us with top quality rods and flies and took turns to row us out onto the lake. When we weren't on the lake we would be hanging around the large cabin, which had been newly constructed on the lakeshore. It was fantastically equipped with the full range of kitchen appliances as well as massive amounts of food and drink. The gamekeepers also lit a fire immediately outside the cabin even though it wasn't particularly cold.

When it came time for the boys to go off quad biking, I was quite happy to stay with the girls at the lake. We caught at least a couple of fish each and I will always remember the look of, almost childlike, joy on Rosie's face when she landed a catch. Even in her, rather cumbersome, fishing gear she managed to look slender, petite and delicious. Jilly also seemed to be happy and, most importantly to me, carefree. Over the years she had taken her career and herself increasingly seriously. It was nice to see her relax. The three wives, none of whom had ever fished before, had a wonderful time. They were wholehearted, friendly and good company. We had a late lunch at the cabin with plenty of good food and wine, got a bit drunk, had a bit of a snooze and then fished a bit more. It was 6.30 p.m. and beginning to get dark when we left the lake. Everyone was in good spirits and we sang songs in the back of the Landrover on the way back to the Cottage.

Back at the Cottage, we were greeted by Mark and his fellow quad bikers. They had obviously heard us singing as we approached the house and when we got inside I got the sense that they hadn't had quite as good a time quad biking as we'd had fishing. They seemed to be a bit resentful. When I say they, I mean, of course, Mark. The ex-cricketers, Phil, Chris and Robbie seemed delighted that their 'other halves' had enjoyed their day and heartily congratulated everyone on their successful catch. Mark made a great show of fussing over the wives while studiously ignoring Rosie, Jilly and me. I could always tell when Mark was pissed off and I knew him well enough to know why. He needed to be the best host, leading the most important guests on the best activity. And whilst he was frequently the person who kept others waiting, he was not happy to be kept waiting himself.

Even though it was only 7 p.m., the boys had obviously been back for some time because they had showered and changed for the evening. Mark announced that the fishing party needed to shower and be in the drawing room within half an hour because pre-dinner drinks were being served at 7.30 p.m. sharp. Jilly and the wives immediately went upstairs to get ready for dinner while Rosie and I remained chatting with the quad bike party. They were very friendly and all of them thanked Rosie and I for entertaining their other halves. Rosie then made her excuses and left the room followed by Mark. I stayed chatting for a while as I knew that Jilly would probably still be in the shower and I thought it best if someone kept Phil, Chris and Robbie entertained. After a few minutes, one of the cricketers, I think it was Phil, said I'd better go and have my shower, "otherwise you'll be late and will get in trouble with Mark." He said this with a big smile on his face. He obviously knew Mark quite well.

As I reached the top of the stairs on the way to the bedroom allocated to Jilly and I, I heard angry voices coming from the direction of Mark and Rosie's room.

"Are you deliberately trying to embarrass me, Rosie?" screamed Mark.

"What do you mean?" Rosie said, hesitantly.

"You know exactly what I mean. You're just fucking rude. This weekend is not all about you and your friends. We've got guests, you know. Those guys are important to the business that I slave over to give you and the kids a better life."

"I'm sorry," said Rosie, quietly.

"Fuck sorry, just don't ever humiliate me by keeping my business contacts waiting again."

"Mark, they didn't seem to mind. In fact they were very relaxed talking to Tom and I."

"Just because they're not fucking rude like you, doesn't mean that it's okay to keep them hanging about until you can be bothered to turn up."

I suppose I shouldn't have paused at the top of the stairs to listen to the argument between Rosie and Mark, but my voyeuristic tendencies got the better of me. I was just about to move towards my bedroom when, to my surprise, Rosie tried to defend herself.

"Look Mark, you're not the only one who was entertaining guests this afternoon. Tom, Jilly and I were doing our bit as well."

"Fuck off," spat Mark. "You're an ignorant bitch. Now get ready and be downstairs in ten minutes."

I was quite shocked by Mark's language. I knew he was capable of speaking to Rosie in an offhand and dismissive way, but I didn't think he would ever be so vicious towards her.

Jilly and I joined the rest of the party in the drawing room just after 7.45 p.m.

"You're late," bellowed Mark.

"Good evening, everybody," I said, smiling and deliberately ignoring him.

Phil came towards me and handed me a gin and tonic, telling me with a mischievous look in the eye that he hoped he hadn't put too much tonic in.

Dinner was a sumptuous affair that everyone enjoyed immensely and Mark was very much the life and soul of the evening. It was only when he casually mentioned to Phil over coffee, that he was looking forward to the game tomorrow that the mood changed. Mark went on to say that he had arranged for a couple of cars to pick 'us' up tomorrow at 9 a.m. so that 'we' will get to the match with plenty of time spare.

"What match?" asked Rosie.

"I told you earlier, darling. Phil, Chris, Robbie and I are going to the Bath vs. Leicester rugby match tomorrow."

"That's the first I've heard of it. What time will you be back?"

"I won't be able to make it back. I'm going to stay in Bath overnight and pick you up in the car early on Monday morning."

"I thought we were staying here until Monday afternoon."

Mark smiled and ended the conversation abruptly.

"Darling, don't make a fuss. I've got to go to a meeting on Monday morning – it's a last minute thing."

Rosie looked crestfallen. It was not unusual for Mark to change their plans with no notice, but on this occasion, he had obviously not even discussed the change of plan with Rosie. I was silently livid. It was bad enough that he had not included me in the earlier activities, but it was humiliating to be excluded from the plans for the second time. Perhaps I should have said something, but I didn't.

# Chapter 5

## *Sunday morning phone call*

The weekend deteriorated further when, early on Sunday morning, Jilly got a call from Roberto Cabrera, the Global Head of Marketing at her company, IPW International. I could hear him clearly even though Jilly was holding her mobile close to her ear. From the tone of his voice I could tell that he didn't think it was presumptuous to call her at the crack of dawn at the weekend, or not to make any attempt at an apology for doing so. Neither did he think that it was unusual to summon an employee to a meeting on a Sunday to help him prepare for an "urgent presentation" he was giving on behalf of the IPW President.

Jilly didn't appear to think it was presumptuous or unusual either and she didn't hesitate to arrange to meet him at his London hotel later that day. As soon as she hung up, and with no hint of regret, never mind an apologetic tone, she announced, "I've got to meet Roberto at noon in London today. He's got to make a presentation to the UK board tomorrow morning and he needs me to help him to prepare. Our company President, Bob Mitchell, was supposed to make the presentation, but he's got to deal with more important issues back in the States."

"Jilly, why didn't you just tell him you're away for the weekend and you can't do it?"

"You don't understand, Tom."

"What don't I understand? You're away for the weekend with friends. Why didn't you just tell him that?"

"It doesn't work that way. I'm Vice President of Marketing in the UK. I've got to help Roberto. If he's doing this on behalf of Bob it has to be good."

When Jilly mentioned the name Bob Mitchell, she did so with a look on her face that indicated that she felt this explained everything. In her mind there was no option but for her to leave for London immediately.

I had actually met Bob a couple of years previously on, what I can only describe as, a bizarre evening of corporate bowing, scraping and fawning. Bob had decided, as a great treat for everyone, to attend the annual IPW International UK Kick-Off. This was a two-day event at which the hierarchy of the UK office celebrated the success of the previous year, outlined to the staff the plans for the next year and talked about how wonderful they all were. On the few occasions I had attended the event I had found it appallingly self-congratulatory, totally insincere and generally nauseating.

The year the President attended however, there was an added element to the proceedings. To my initial amusement and then horror, he acted, with the full collaboration of the UK staff, as if he were some kind of religious prophet or cult leader. Jilly and I were enjoying a pre-dinner drink when I first met 'Big Bad Bob'. He swept into the room flanked by a couple of all-American, clean-cut lackeys and, with no regard for anyone but himself, started to bellow.

"Good evening, ladies and gentlemen and welcome to IPW International's 20th UK Annual Kick-Off."

He then turned to one of Jilly's colleagues and used her to continue his bellowing. "It's so great to see you, Melanie, and to see that you are wearing your long service badge. Melanie has been with the company for eight years and her loyalty pleases me very much."

"Ah, Mike," he went on, without taking a breath, "Mike, you're looking great and I notice that you're wearing, with great pride, your ten year service signet ring. Mike, show the ladies and gentlemen your ring."

My immediate, and perhaps a little juvenile, response to what Bob had said was to burst out laughing. I scanned the room to see if anyone else had picked up on the, what I considered to be, ambiguous instruction for Mike to "show the ladies and gentlemen your ring". I was met with completely blank faces except for Jilly who stared at me with an expression that conveyed both fury and exasperation. I quickly regained my composure and watched, with what I hoped was well-concealed contempt, as Mike toured the room showing off his, rather ridiculous, long-service signet ring.

Later, as Bob roamed around the room, his UK staff appeared to be bowing to him as he addressed them. Bob talked 'at' them for about thirty seconds each. No response was required. They bowed to him repeatedly and then he moved on to the next victim. I knew many of these people and their behaviour shocked me. They had previously seemed to me to be a rational, determined and professional team of people. Now they were bowing and acting as if they were the indentured servants of a medieval lord.

As we made our way to dinner I turned to Jilly, who had also acted in the most demeaning and obsequious way, and said "I can't believe what I've just seen. You were bowing to Bob."

"What do you mean?"

"You, Melanie, Mike and the rest, actually *bowed* to Bob."

"No we didn't."

"Yes you did – I was there. All of you bowed to Bob while he shouted at you."

"Shut up, Tom. People can hear."

Jilly then accused me of being drunk and pleaded with me to be quiet, explaining that this was just the way the corporate world worked. I argued, more quietly this time, that she and the rest of them had been humiliating themselves. I was genuinely confused at what I'd just witnessed. Maybe that's why I'd never really progressed as I'd hoped in the business world.

Things got even more comical when we sat down for dinner. On each of our seats was a piece of paper on which was written, what I initially took to be, a prayer or grace. This, I thought was understandable bearing in mind the mid-west American hierarchy at IPW. On closer inspection however, it was no such thing. It was a two verse, rhyming poem entitled *Bob's Mission Statement*. I read it and had to stop myself laughing out loud for the second time that evening.

*'With strength and fortitude we can hope,*
*To help IPW's customers always cope,*
*And when their IT systems crash,*
*We will prevent them their teeth to gnash.*

*IPW's service teams across the nations,*
*Will always strive to fix workstations,*
*Whether it's Apple, HP or Dell,*
*The odour of success they will smell.'*

Jilly's colleague, Mike, turned to me and began to tell me what a great man President Bob was. He described him as a visionary, and made the ridiculous claim that, during his time in power, Bill Clinton had never made a foreign policy decision without consulting with Bob first. He then asked me what I thought of *Bob's Mission Statement*. I looked at Mike to see if there was any hint of a wry smile on his face. There wasn't. I tried to evade his question, but he pressed me.

"Come on, Tom. If you had to use one word to describe *Bob's Mission Statement* what would it be?"

I paused and then said quietly, "Infantile."

This was met with a hefty kick from Jilly who was sitting opposite me. I quickly laughed off my 'joke' response to Mike and confirmed to him that, although I had only had limited exposure to Bob and his work, it was obvious that, within the IT world, he was indeed, a visionary.

Jilly and I had very different views on the corporate

world. I couldn't bring myself to take it entirely seriously and, although I tried to hide this fact from my colleagues, they probably knew how I felt. I would never have cut my weekend short for what I saw as an unnecessary meeting in London. With Jilly however, work had always come first and I suppose that was why she had done so well. Whereas I probably wouldn't have taken a call from my boss on a Sunday morning, Jilly would always have done so. Once her boss had made it clear that her presence in London was required there was never a doubt in her mind that she would leave Butterfield Cottage early.

# Chapter 6

## *Jilly's betrayal*

Jilly was gone by 9.30 a.m. that morning and I was left to my own devices. I was annoyed that she had gone so willingly and just a little worried about her meeting her boss at his London hotel. I had met Roberto Cabrera many times and I didn't trust Jilly with him. He was very flirty with her and she flirted back with huge enthusiasm. She did this despite the fact that she knew it made me feel very uncomfortable. It made me feel uncomfortable for a very good reason. While I had got used to the fact that Jilly had always flirted with almost every man she came into contact with, in more recent times she had done a lot more than just flirt.

Jilly had returned to work a few years after the birth of our second son, Sam. While it was true that we were struggling with only my salary coming in and therefore her return to work was necessary, it was also true that Jilly was bored at home and desperately wanted to return to the cut and thrust of the workplace. She loved her job in marketing and particularly loved working with the sales force. I always got the impression that she wasn't that popular within the marketing department, which was staffed predominately by women, but she was extremely popular within the sales department, which was staffed almost exclusively by men.

A year or so after Jilly returned to work she was rewarded for hitting her targets, with an all-expenses-paid trip for the two of us to Las Vegas. I never quite understood how someone in marketing could hit targets, but I wasn't complaining and was excited as we assembled at Heathrow, along with eighty or so others for, what had been billed by the company as, 'the trip of a lifetime.' Jilly and I were in our late thirties at this time and although I considered us to still be a relatively young couple, when we met her colleagues and their partners at Heathrow, I was surprised by how much younger so many of them were. Jilly and I were very much in the category of elder statesmen and I remember thinking, for probably the first time in my life, that I was getting on a bit. Maybe this was how Jilly felt. Maybe that was why she did what she did.

When we arrived in Las Vegas, I was stunned by the audacity of the city. I had been expecting it to be a bit tacky, cheap and ridiculous, and it was. But it was also fabulous, outrageous and very, very exciting. My first sighting of the Strip made me burst out laughing. The first thing that caught my eye was the New York Hotel, the outline of which perfectly mirrored the Manhattan skyline. The hotel had a roller coaster, which ran through the middle of it. We ate there on our first evening in Las Vegas and it not only served up top quality food, but also enabled parents to eat lavishly while their kids flew through the air just a few feet above them on one of the roller coaster loops. Further up the Strip was The Bellagio, a luxury hotel with a huge lake outside it. The lake had hundreds of fountains running across the middle of it. The fountains would spring into life, illuminated by red, white and blue lights, shooting water high into the air perfectly in time with *Viva Las Vegas* or *God Bless America*, which blasted out from enormous speakers. Further up the Strip was a replica of the Eiffel Tower, which was three quarters of the size of the real thing, a pirate ship and a wild array of neon lights that seemed to shine brighter than the sun. I was appalled by Las Vegas and absolutely loved it at the same time.

There was a gala dinner on the second night of our stay at the Venetian Hotel. We travelled to our dining experience in gondolas, which floated along fake canals inside the hotel complex. Above our heads was a perfect replica of the Venetian night sky. It shouldn't have worked, but it did. At pre-dinner drinks there was a huge buzz of excitement and everybody seemed genuinely happy. Early on in the evening, I noticed Jilly's outrageous flirting with her colleagues, but initially didn't really think anything of it. It was par for the course with Jilly. I was, however, made a bit uneasy by the attention she was showing to one particularly handsome, young salesman.

Jilly had complained after the birth of our second son that she felt 'mumsy'. I had pointed out that she should feel this way, as she had just become a mother for the second time. My simple statement was met with a tirade of abuse about my insensitivity and the fact that, although I might want to accept being middle-aged, she most certainly wasn't going to. After things calmed down a bit, Jilly explained, a little more calmly, and with a few tears, that while she loved being a mother she also wanted to look and feel like an attractive woman. She wanted to have a flat stomach again, to lose the weight she had put on around her hips and the tops of her legs and, most importantly, to feel that her breasts were not just a "milk factory". She also wanted to know that I fancied her as much as I had before she had children. At the time, I took this at face value, but I was shortly going to come to the conclusion that it wasn't just me she wanted to fancy her. No, she wanted to know that the effect that she'd always had on all red-blooded men between the ages of eighteen and thirty was not a thing of the past.

I was struck, before we left our hotel room to make our way to the dinner, by just how gorgeous Jilly looked. She was wearing a black cocktail dress, cut above the knee so that it showed off her fantastically long, slim legs and her newly flat stomach. Unlike a lot of the younger women, Jilly did not feel the need to wear a dress that revealed her cleavage, but somehow that made her look all the more sexy. Before we left our room, I did manage to compliment her, but perhaps I should have made more of a fuss. That was certainly what Nick, the dashing, young salesman, did.

Nick was over six foot, probably about twenty-eight and very good-looking in a boyish type of way. He had a thick, dark mane of hair, which, although reasonably long, seemed to defy gravity. It sat lustrously on the top of his head making him look even taller than he was.

Slim-hipped and broad-shouldered, he had a swimmer's physique and looked very comfortable and confident in his own skin. Although I was only a few inches shorter than him, I felt a bit dumpy in comparison. I hadn't let myself go entirely, but there had been a certain thickening around the waist and a greying and thinning of the hair around my temples. By comparison to Nick, I suppose I looked a bit jaded.

After Nick had finished showering Jilly with, what I thought, were over the top compliments, she moved towards him and kissed him on the cheek. She kissed him a little bit too close to his lips, I thought, and lingered just a little bit too long on his cheek. She then snaked her right arm under his jacket and around the small of his back. He, in turn, put his arm around her lower back and rested the palm of his hand on her hipbone while his fingers rested gently on her stomach. At dinner he was seated at a different table to Jilly and I and, although she flirted with all the men on our table, I felt a lot more comfortable and relaxed without Nick in attendance. There were a couple of speeches after dinner which consisted of various 'bigwigs' banging on about how great they were, how IPW was wonderful and how with everyone's help even greater things would be achieved in the future. I can't remember much of the content of the speeches, other than that there was mention of a helicopter trip to the Grand Canyon the next morning for those of us who were interested. Jilly and I agreed that the trip was not to be missed and signed up to go.

After dinner the tables were cleared away and a local rock band began playing. Usually, it is fair to say, 'local rock bands' are pretty average, but this was Las Vegas and, perhaps unsurprisingly, they were brilliant. The lead singer must have been in his mid-sixties, but he could certainly bang out a great song and he got everybody up onto the dance floor almost immediately. I hadn't expected it, but I was having a great night. This was only slightly spoilt at the end of the evening when the band played some much slower rock ballads. The music was great, but it allowed Nick, who I hadn't seen for a couple of hours, to appear from nowhere and ask Jilly to dance. Most people were at least a little bit tipsy by this stage and thankfully I don't think they noticed just how intimate Nick and Jilly were becoming. That at least saved me from a publicly humiliating situation, but it didn't stop me from raging with jealousy. Jilly held Nick very close to her as they danced and looked up at him in, what I thought was, an adoring way. I was quite relieved when the band played their last song and I could legitimately prise Jilly from Nick's arms.

When we got upstairs to our room, I let Jilly know exactly what I thought of her.

"You made a bit of spectacle of yourself tonight."

"What do you mean?" Jilly replied in, what I considered to be, a mock innocent way.

"You were all over him."

"All over who?"

I've got to admit this provocatively stupid question made me very angry.

"Oh come on, Jilly, you know who. As soon as you saw Nick you had your hands all over him and then when you were slow dancing with him at the end you looked like you were enjoying it far too much."

"Don't be pathetic, Tom. We're good friends that's all. He's a rising star at IPW and I find him really good company. Get over yourself."

At various times in our relationship, Jilly had made me feel inadequate, either by making it obvious she found someone else attractive or by pointedly admiring the business talents of a friend or colleague. In this case, she was doing both. I should have challenged her further, but experience told me that she would just laugh at me. It was this powerlessness to make an impact on her that frustrated me most.

I retreated to the far reaches of the room to avoid Jilly in case I lost the plot completely. Fortunately, this was made possible by the fact that our room was ridiculously big. We had been told, when we checked in, that our suite had an area of over a thousand square feet. This description didn't really mean much to me, but when we got to our room I was actually shocked by the size of it. There were three distinct bedroom sections with a king-sized bed in each, two bathrooms, a sitting room and a study. It was so large that it was easier to phone someone on the far side of the room than actually talk to them. We slept in separate beds that night.

In the morning, I was woken by Jilly very early so that we could shower before our helicopter trip to the Grand Canyon. Despite our row the previous night, and a slight hangover, I was feeling pretty excited about the trip. Jilly was also complaining of a hangover and she said that she hoped having a shower would make her feel a bit more human. She may have been complaining about feeling ill, but when she emerged from the shower she looked absolutely gorgeous. Her wet hair was brushed back and was sleek against her head and back. She obviously had no make-up on and her natural beauty was striking. Her bright, blue eyes needed no enhancement from mascara or eyeliner and her slightly tanned skin had a perfect golden hue to it. She had wrapped a small towel around her waist, which meant her full, plump breasts were on glorious display. I moved towards her, our little disagreement of the night before forgotten, at least by me, cupped her left breast in my right hand and went to kiss her. She pushed me away gently and said she felt too hungover and ill for that sort of thing.

I was pretty frustrated. She said that although she hadn't actually been sick, she was feeling so ill that she thought she might be and that, perhaps, she shouldn't go on the trip to The Grand Canyon. My frustration at not being able to fondle her breasts and perhaps have my way with her before we set off, was now compounded by the disappointment of realising that we might not be going to the Grand Canyon after all.

"Maybe you'll feel a bit better once you've had some breakfast?" I said, encouragingly.

"I couldn't even think about eating. I think I need to lie down."

"Damn, I was really looking forward to today."

"You can still go."

"I'm not going without you. I don't know these people and I don't want to be wandering around by myself all day, looking like a spare part."

"Don't be ridiculous, there's lots of singles on the trip. You'll be fine. Just because I'm going to miss out doesn't mean that we both should."

"Are you sure you'll be alright?"

"After a couple of hours sleep I'll be fine. You go."

I didn't need much persuasion to be honest and, after a few more weak protestations, off I went.

—

At breakfast, I bumped into a few familiar faces from the night before. They were all friendly and concerned about Jilly after I explained the situation. Jilly was right, while there were mostly couples on the trip, there were plenty of singles at breakfast. When the trip leader appeared, I soon forgot about the disappointment of Jilly not being able to make it and began to look forward to the day's activities. The trip leader went through the itinerary for the day and then said we would be leaving in ten minutes. We were advised to check that we had sun cream, cameras and some money for lunch, as this was not being paid for. I, like an idiot, had forgotten my camera. I excused myself from the breakfast table and made my way back to the room. I was determined that I would take some decent photos to show Jilly on my return.

I entered the room as quietly as possible because I thought Jilly would probably have gone back to sleep. As soon as I got inside, I could hear that Jilly was still awake. At first I mistook the groaning I could hear as Jilly being sick, but as I passed the first bedroom area and moved into the open-plan sitting room, the groaning took on a much more rhythmical tone. I stopped in my tracks and listened. At first I don't think I could actually compute what was happening. I had only left the room twenty-five minutes earlier and, while I was excited about the helicopter trip to the Grand Canyon, I was also genuinely concerned about Jilly. It was obvious what was happening, but I still couldn't believe it.

As I walked further into the suite I caught sight of Jilly. She was in the bed nearest to the window and was sitting astride an unknown figure with her back to me. I remember staring at her lightly muscled shoulders and beautifully tapered waist, I was transfixed as she moved, ever more urgently, up and down and her groaning became clearly identifiable as moaning. My shock turned to fascination and then horror as she arched her back and ground herself onto the figure below her. As she repeatedly raised her bottom and began driving downward with her hips, her moans turned to high-pitched squeals.

At last I came to my senses and calmly said, "Hi Jilly, I forgot my camera."

For just a moment Jilly continued grinding up and down and then suddenly rolled away from the figure beneath her. She instantly grabbed at the bed sheets and covered herself with them, simultaneously uncovering the figure beneath her. Even at the time, I remember thinking that it was odd that her first reaction was to cover herself up while exposing Nick to me in all his glory. He continued to lie on the bed while Jilly moved quickly towards me saying she was sorry. As she reached me, she stretched out an arm and tried to put her hand to my face. I pushed her hand away and continued staring at Nick. He seemed to lie there for an eternity before languidly getting to his feet and walking slowly to the chair where he had left his clothes. He dressed hurriedly and then without a word walked calmly past me, through the suite and out into the corridor.

# Chapter 7

## *Sunday with Rosie*

I went down for breakfast as soon as Jilly had left for London. I was very disappointed that she had gone, but at the same time I was determined to make the most of the rest of my stay in Wiltshire. When I arrived in the breakfast room Rosie was seated at the table. I was pleased to see her, but felt sure that she would say that Mark had arranged for her to go back to London later that day. In fact, Mark had decided to stick to his plan to pick Rosie up very early on Monday morning on his way back home. It suddenly occurred to me that although I had known Rosie for nearly thirty years, I had not spent any significant time alone with her. I was looking forward to spending the whole day with my old friend.

We decided that just because our other halves had abandoned us, we would be stupid to waste the opportunity to enjoy the facilities at Butterfield Cottage. We would go for a swim after breakfast, then for a long walk, have lunch sent up to the lodge at the lake, shoot some clays in the afternoon, have a slap-up dinner and watch a good film in the evening. Rosie explained to me that Mark only liked to watch action films and asked if we could watch a 'rom-com'. I was only too happy to agree that this was the way to go. I would never have admitted it to Mark, but action films bored me, while a little bit of romance was right up my soft-hearted street.

The swimming pool complex at the Cottage was a relatively recent addition. It was situated in a newly-converted barn, which was connected via an enclosed, glass walkway to the main house. I got to the complex before Rosie and had a chance to look around before she arrived. Like everything else at Butterfield Cottage it had been very tastefully designed. At the near end were the changing rooms, a fully fitted sauna and an exercise pool with swim jets. Along one side of the main pool were a series of loungers and two huge, glass windows, which could be opened to provide access to an outside terrace and the lawn beyond. At the far end of the barn there was a bar area. By the time Rosie joined me, I'd had a good look around and was able to give her a guided tour. She didn't seem to be as impressed with our surroundings as I was. I suddenly realised that she and Mark probably stayed in places like this all the time and to her it was pretty normal. I was a bit embarrassed by my 'kid in a sweet shop' excitement and quickly suggested that we get in the pool.

Rosie and I came out of our respective changing rooms simultaneously. I rarely seemed to have time to go to the gym, but I considered myself to be in reasonable shape – a bit thick around the waist perhaps, but nothing that a bit of 'sucking in' couldn't mostly disguise. I had also splashed myself with some cold water before checking myself in the mirror and leaving the men's changing room. The cold water had the desired effect of tightening up the skin around my chest and arms and I remember thinking I looked at least passable. Rosie on the other hand looked, if anything, even slighter than she had all those years ago in Cornwall. I made sure that I held her gaze as she emerged from her changing room so that she didn't think I was looking her up and down too obviously, but I was able to discern quite a lot without being obvious. She wore a white, one-piece swimming costume, which showed off all the little curves and bumps of her body. We dived into the pool together, surfaced for air and decided that we should do half an hour of lengths in order that we could exercise away the excesses of the last couple of days. We swam side by side and it felt good. I was pleased to be taking some exercise and I was pleased to be with Rosie. In fact I remember being more than pleased to be with Rosie, I struggled to think at the time as to how I was feeling but decided that the best description, odd as it might sound, was thrilled.

After we had finished our lengths, Rosie was in a playful mood. She challenged me to see if I could do a length underwater and, after I completed nearly two, she started to tease me.

"Wow, you're really great, Tom. You did nearly two lengths, you're my hero."

I joined in saying, "Yes, I guess I am kinda special and manly. Now, little lady, why don't you see what you can do."

Rosie got out of the pool and took as long a run-up as possible and dived in. I watched intently as she propelled her lithe body gracefully through the water. She easily completed two lengths and popped out of the water with a huge smile on her face. She raised her arms into the air and started chanting, "Rosie is great. Rosie is great. Rosie is great." When she'd finished chanting her own name, we both burst out laughing.

We had competitions to see who could do the most lengths without using their legs, races with me doing breaststroke and her front crawl and, in between, gave each other marks out of ten for our most stylish dives. We spent a couple of hours in the pool and we laughed and laughed. It was joyful. When we finally decided that it was time to get out of the pool, Rosie was shivering slightly and looked absolutely stunning. Her dark hair was swept back off her face and was sleek to her head. For the first time I noticed that her ears slightly stuck out and that, combined with her shivering, made her look sweet and innocent. As she got out of the pool, I got a chance to have a proper look at her body and there was nothing sweet or innocent about that. Her one-piece swimsuit clung to her athletic body in the most provocative and sexy way possible. Now that it was wet, her swimming costume was slightly see-through and the outline of her perfect breasts was very obvious. Her nipples were dark against both her skin and the white of the costume. The material also clung semi-transparently to her stomach and hips. Rosie, I'm pretty sure, was totally unaware of exactly how enticing she looked or indeed that I was studying her so intently.

After showering and dressing, we set off on our walk to the lake. It would take at least an hour to get there, but the reward would be the fabulous late lunch that I was sure would be waiting for us at the lodge by the lake. Rosie had managed to find a hat in the boot room, which perfectly complemented her walking gear. It was one of those Australian Bush Hats which had become popular over the previous few years and I was struck by how, even dressed in baggy walking gear, Rosie managed to look incredibly stylish. As we walked, we talked and laughed and talked a bit more. Rosie told me she was looking to do something beyond looking after the kids and going to charity lunches. She said that Mark wasn't keen on her working, partly because she wasn't "qualified or experienced enough to do anything worthwhile" and partly because there was "nothing more worthwhile than looking after the kids." Rosie also explained that Mark considered the charity lunches a useful way for her to cultivate friendships with the wives of people he wanted to network with. She seemed resigned to the fact that, at least until the children were grown up, she was destined to fulfil the role of housewife and mother and nothing much else.

We touched briefly on the hopes and ambitions that I had for my career. It was a half-hearted conversation. It is difficult to convince someone else of your commitment to the 'corporate' cause when you haven't been able to convince yourself. We quickly moved on to the subject of education and our children and their lives, before reminiscing about our youth and our first meeting in Cornwall. Rosie had some pretty clear memories of that first meeting.

"You completely ignored me that first year in Cornwall. You only seemed interested in drinking, smoking and messing about with the boys. Patrick's little sister wasn't on your radar."

"Rosie, you were the only thing on my radar"

"What?"

"I fancied you rotten from the first moment I saw you."

"No you didn't, Tom. You completely ignored me. I remember sitting on a wall and sharing a cigarette with you and you couldn't even be bothered to speak to me."

"It wasn't that I couldn't be bothered, it was that I liked you so much that I couldn't think of anything to say that wasn't completely stupid."

"I had no idea."

"Well, you do now. What did you think of me?"

"I really liked you, but I just imagined that you never spoke to me because you thought I was just a silly kid."

I was a mixture of happy and frustrated. I was happy that, for the first time, Rosie actually confirmed that she had some feelings for me, but frustrated that I hadn't read the signals, didn't take the risk and that, the next year, Mark had done exactly what I should have done. What a fool. Rosie broke my train of thought by announcing that she was absolutely starving. I agreed and told her that we were no more than ten minutes from the lodge and a slap-up lunch. At that moment the skies opened and the rain came pouring down. It had been threatening all day and when it started it was the type of heavy rain that drenched you almost immediately. When we got to our destination we were both soaking wet.

Thankfully, the lodge was equipped with a shower, a wood burner and a fully stocked fridge. We could, therefore, get out of our sodden clothes, get warm and satiate our hunger. While Rosie showered, I went outside to get logs for the wood burner. By the time she emerged I was more than ready to get in the shower myself. Rosie had obviously found some freshly laundered spare clothes and she looked great in them. She was wearing some fluffy green socks, black leggings and a Butterfield Cottage sweatshirt. While I went for a shower, Rosie said she would go to the kitchen area to see what had been prepared for our lunch. By the time I appeared in the kitchen, wearing some decidedly unflattering elephant cords and a twittish, checked shirt, Rosie had laid out the perfect picnic lunch.

Lunch was an eclectic mix of locally-sourced pork pies, Scotch eggs, quails' eggs, cucumber sandwiches, quiche, cold asparagus in vinaigrette, handmade pasta salad, flatbread, olives and hummus. The best Chablis I have ever tasted complemented all of this. Rosie picked at the food although she claimed to have thoroughly enjoyed it, and I didn't eat that much so that I had room for the strawberries and cream that would be our pudding. I noticed that, although Rosie ate sparingly, she didn't hold back when it came to the Chablis. We were both a little 'squiffy' by the time we finished lunch.

We decided that we were a bit too tired and certainly a bit too tipsy to go clay pigeon shooting. I suggested that perhaps, as the lodge was so comfortable, we should stay for a few hours. Our plan was to get the wood burner going and watch a film on the flat screen TV that had thoughtfully been provided. We tidied away the remains of our lunch and, although we didn't have to, decided to wash up. We chatted away as we stood at the sink, Rosie washing and me drying, and the conversation turned to Jilly and me.

"You and Jilly seem to be getting on really well."

"We are, I think. It took me a while to get over what happened in Las Vegas, and I don't think I'll ever trust her fully again, but things are pretty good."

"Oh I'm so sorry, Tom. I didn't mean to bring up the past, I know how awful that was for you."

"Don't worry, it happened and I've come to terms with it. I don't think she'd ever do it again because she knows that, if she did, that would be the end."

I had confided in Mark about what had happened in Las Vegas and I wondered if he had told Rosie exactly what went on. I'd hoped not, but on the other hand I couldn't imagine him not describing each and every detail to Rosie. Mark had actually been almost totally unsympathetic when I told him. He had basically said that it was my fault for being a "pushover." I didn't know what he meant at first, but he went on to explain, in pretty brutal terms, his theory.

"Look mate, if you run around after your wife making sure she gets everything she wants and telling the world, including her, that you would never even think of fucking anyone else, then guess what? She'll just take you for granted and fuck about herself."

I'd argued that his theory was rubbish, but he challenged me to name the three worst behaved men he knew and asked if I thought their wives had ever been unfaithful to them. The worst behaved man I knew was Mark. Marriage had not interrupted his pursuit of women at all. He'd even had a fairly serious relationship with one of Rosie's friends for three months either side of their wedding day. As his Best Man, I was even charged with the responsibility of making sure "the mad bitch" didn't turn up on the big day and make a scene. This wasn't an isolated incident either. Mark had a series of girlfriends and one-night stands throughout his married life, and I happened to know that he had spent a weekend in Rome with a woman within the last few weeks. Mark had always been completely open with me about his behaviour and correctly predicted that he would be one of my three worst behaved men.

"Bearing in mind the sheltered fucking life that you live, I would imagine that you think my behaviour is pretty bad. Well, tell me, do you think Rosie's ever fucked about?"

"No Mark, but Rosie doesn't know what you get up to, so that's not the reason she stays faithful to you."

"Of course she fucking knows. She might not know names and dates, but she knows it happens. She just chooses to ignore it."

Mark's argument didn't really make sense to me, but it was quite obvious that he was completely convinced that he was right and that I had brought Jilly's infidelity upon myself.

As Rosie and I stood at the sink and dried the remaining dishes, I changed the subject and explained to her that the only significant problem Jilly and I had these days was money, or to be more precise, the lack of it. The school fees were crippling us and while there was a possibility that Jilly might earn significantly more over the coming years, it was unlikely to happen quickly enough to help.

"Not a problem that you and Mark have," I noted.

"No, I suppose not."

"Things seem pretty good for you and Mark. Plenty of money, two lovely kids and you both seem really happy."

Rosie didn't reply at first, she just turned to me and stared. She was pale and her lower lip was quivering. I stared back at her, waiting for her to say something. Her eyes filled with tears and she looked at me with an utterly defeated look on her face. The tears rolled down her cheeks and she began to sob. At first, I did nothing. I hadn't seen this coming at all. I moved slowly towards Rosie, not sure what to do. Her sobs became more pronounced until they became convulsions and gasps. I reached out towards her, put my hand on her shoulder and asked her in a soft voice, "What's wrong, Rosie?"

She gasped for air and repeated just one word, "I'm, I'm, I'm—"

"It's okay, Rosie. Stay calm and breathe."

I held her face gently between my hands and, as calmly as I could, urged her to relax. I was becoming increasingly concerned as Rosie was now hyperventilating, but she seemed determined to speak.

"I'm— I'm—I'm... so unhappy."

"Don't talk, Rosie, just breathe. Slow, deep breaths. That's it."

She gradually began to breathe more regularly and once she had calmed down sufficiently I pulled her towards me and put my arms around her. She nestled her head into my chest and, with her arms hanging limply from her sides, she continued to take deep, slow breaths. I hadn't seen anybody hyperventilate to the point of collapse before and I was really shocked. I held her for what seemed an eternity, but was probably just a minute or so, and we breathed together. Eventually, Rosie leaned back and looked up at me. I took my arms away from her and she whispered, "I'm sorry, Tom."

"Sorry for what?"

"Sorry for being such an idiot."

We walked over to the sofa and sat down together. I smiled at her and put my arm back around her shoulders and she rested her head against me. We sat in silence for quite a while. I couldn't make up my mind whether to press her for more information or whether to let her talk in her own time. I finally came to the conclusion that my concern and curiosity meant that I had to ask her.

"If you don't want to talk about it I'll understand, Rosie. But if you're that unhappy you really should talk to someone."

"Do you mean a shrink?"

"No, no. I mean a friend."

"I don't think any of my friends would understand. As you said, my life seems perfect. Perfect, that is, to everyone but me. I would just sound selfish and spoilt. The only person who would understand is you and I can't talk to you because you're Mark's best friend."

"I'm your friend as well, Rosie, and you can trust me completely. I would never repeat anything you say to Mark."

There was a long silence between the two of us. After a couple of minutes she made an attempt to sit up straighter and I took this as a cue to take my arm from around her shoulders. She moved along the sofa and turned towards me. She smiled weakly and I could see the tears welling up in her eyes again. When she eventually spoke, it was like a dam had burst. The words came flooding out.

"I just feel like I'm a non-person. I haven't got any control over my life at all. Mark decides who we socialise with, when and where we go on holiday, which schools the boys go to, whether I can work or not, who I can like, what I should wear and even what I should think. I'm glad we came here for the weekend with you and Jilly, but we didn't talk about it, Mark just told me we were coming and that I needed to get the boys looked after. I've given up seeing some of my old friends because Mark refuses to come with me and if I try to discuss it with him he just loses his temper. I can't commit to anything without asking him first and he's told me that I mustn't arrange anything in case I am needed at a business function."

Rosie started sobbing again and I shuffled towards her and put my arms around her once more. She looked up at me and raw emotion poured out of her.

"He doesn't even talk to me anymore. If he's not away on business, he comes home in a filthy mood, eats his dinner in silence and then goes straight to bed. He is constantly on his mobile when we do spend time together and has a fit if I suggest that he turns it off. If he does communicate with me, it's by text when he's at work and then only to tell me to do something or to tell me that my presence is required somewhere. He doesn't even seem interested in me physically any more. I can't remember the last time we made love."

I looked at Rosie and although I knew I should have been thinking of some sympathetic words to say to her, all I could really think about was how gorgeous she looked. Even with her red eyes and mascara streaked down her cheeks, she was more beautiful to me than she had ever been. I had to stop myself from leaning forward and kissing her. Her comment about sex, or the lack of it, surprised me on a couple of levels. Firstly, who wouldn't want to make love to this exquisite creature as often as possible. Secondly, Mark had always been highly-sexed and had, in the recent past, given me the distinct impression that his sex life with Rosie was very healthy.

I knew that Mark had had a couple of fairly serious affairs in recent years, but it hadn't occurred to me that these affected his relationship with Rosie. Mark had always 'played away' and had made it quite clear to me that he thought it was very odd that I didn't. Perhaps I should have said something to Rosie years ago, but I had taken the view that it was none of my business. It would also have made me feel incredibly disloyal to my oldest friend if I had told anyone, let alone Rosie, what I knew. I tried to reassure her.

"I'm sure Mark loves you. He's probably just incredibly busy and stressed. Things will get better, they usually do."

"I hope you're right, Tom, because I don't think I can stand being completely ignored for much longer."

Rosie and I spent the rest of the afternoon curled up on the sofa watching Clarke Gable romance Claudette Colbert in *It Happened One Night*. The only interruptions we had to, what was to me at least, a perfect afternoon, was the occasional visit from a member of staff. Part of their job was obviously to make sure that guests were continually made to feel that if they wanted for anything, they would get it. We sat very close to each other with Rosie draping various limbs around me. I don't know whether she was concentrating on the film, but I certainly couldn't. I was constantly trying to seem relaxed while this beautiful woman lounged next to me. She was obviously very relaxed because even when the staff came in to see if there was anything we wanted, she made no attempt to untangle herself from me. When the film ended, Rosie turned towards me on the sofa put her arms around me, held me close to her and kissed me on the cheek.

"Thanks, Tom."

"Thanks for what?"

"Thanks for listening, thanks for looking after me and thanks for being my friend. I promise I won't bore you with my problems over dinner."

—

We drank quite a lot over dinner, or at least I did. Rosie only drank a couple of glasses of wine, but rather than making her morose or unhappy as it had over lunch, she seemed completely relaxed and at ease. We both smiled and laughed a lot and I felt that I had never been closer to her. We had decided that it would be ridiculous to eat in the main dining room as the table was so enormous and so we ate in the kitchen. We had also told the cook to make something simple for us and to tell the rest of the staff to have the evening off. Once the cook had left, we were completely alone in the house.

After supper, Rosie suggested that we go outside for a cigarette. Rosie had given up smoking several years earlier, so I was surprised that the suggestion came from her. Rosie took a cigarette from my packet and suggested that we share it, as she didn't want a whole one. As I lit the cigarette, I couldn't help but notice once again how beautiful she was. Her flawless complexion, her naturally pouting lips and gorgeous green-brown eyes. After a couple of drags, Rosie offered the cigarette to me. She had been very tactile over dinner but I couldn't work out whether she was flirting. Sharing a cigarette, however, convinced me that I wasn't just hoping that she felt something for me, she was giving me clear signals. I took the cigarette from her and put it to my lips. It was damp from her lips and I got the same electric shock as I had got all those years ago in Cornwall. I didn't think I was still capable of reacting in such a way.

I was hoping that Rosie would move towards me and we would kiss, but of course that wasn't going to happen. She was not the type to make the first move. It was up to me, but I just couldn't seem to find the right moment. All of a sudden the cigarette was finished and Rosie suggested we go back inside, as it was getting a bit cold. She linked arms with me and, as we walked through the kitchen door, I was almost bursting with lust and frustration. I had spent the whole day with a woman I'd been in love with for nearly thirty years. She had trusted me enough to confide her most intimate feelings. She had leant against me, touched me and shared a cigarette with me and still, I hadn't made my move. How many more signals could she give me without spelling it out letter by letter? As we sat back down at the kitchen table, I came to the conclusion that I had no more balls as a forty-six year old man than I had as an eighteen year old boy. I was never going to get the girl.

Twenty minutes later, we were back in our respective bedrooms. Rosie had probably decided that I was never going to make a move. She said she was tired, and that she had better go to bed as Mark was picking her up very early the next morning on his way back from Bath.

As I sat there, in the dark, in my bedroom, I blamed Mark and then Rosie and finally myself for not taking my opportunity to progress things further with Rosie. Through gritted teeth I started talking silently to myself.

*Typical of that bastard Mark to get in the way of Rosie and me. Even when he's miles away he exerts his influence and his power over people. He fucks about, he's cruel to Rosie, he treats me like shit but still he makes the decisions. I want Rosie. She wants me. But even in his absence he's still controlling everybody and everything.*

My internalised ranting continued with: *But Rosie's got to take some blame hasn't she? Why couldn't she just make the move? She must know how I feel. I told her earlier how I felt about her when we were kids. She knows Jilly and I have been through tough times and surely she must realise that Mark has betrayed her over and over again. Why couldn't she take the initiative and for once in her life take a risk with me?*

I quickly realised, of course, that I should be blaming myself. There was only one person that I should be angry with and that was me, and I was very angry with my lack of courage. It had thwarted me my whole life. Whenever it mattered I had chickened out, not once but over and over again. It was then that I knew with a certainty that I wasn't going to chicken out this time. This time I was going to take a risk, this time I was going to get the girl. I got to my feet and went to the bathroom, undressed, put on my bathrobe and cleaned my teeth. I then checked my reflection in the mirror and before I could change my mind I left my room and headed for Rosie's. I felt powerful, very powerful and I knew that this was what I needed to do. As I approached her room, I breathed in deeply through my nostrils and clenched and unclenched my fists to relieve my tension. I reached her door, knocked very gently and moved inside.

I stood stock-still inside Rosie's room for a few seconds in order that my eyes could get used to the darkness. I had left the door slightly ajar, so I knew that Rosie, if awake, would be able to see me. I said nothing and heard nothing except for my heart thumping in my chest. As my eyes adjusted to the darkness, I could see that she was awake and sitting up in her bed. I was half expecting her to scream or at least ask me what I wanted, but she remained silent. After what seemed like an eternity, but was probably only a few seconds, I took a deep breath and moved towards her bed. I sat down beside her, put my hand to her face and caressed her. I slowly pushed her down onto the bed, cupped her face in my hands and kissed her gently on the lips. I felt her mouth open and slowly I began to explore her lips and mouth. Kissing her was everything I had ever imagined. Her lips were incredibly soft. I was fully aroused and desperate to be inside her but I had waited so long for this moment that I knew I would rush nothing. I loved her and was going to make love to her, not just have sex.

I moved from her lips to the nape of her neck and drank in the smell and taste of her. As I kissed her I slid the duvet cover down to her waist and rested my hand on her belly. I stopped kissing her for a moment to look at her face, breasts and stomach. There was just enough light coming from the hallway for me to see every contour and crease. Her breasts were small and her hipbones protruded above her convex belly. She looked even better than I had imagined and I fixed my gaze on her eyes before kissing her again on the lips and then moving to her neck and finally her breasts. As I did this, I slipped my hand under the duvet and between her legs. She parted her legs and smiled coquettishly.

By now I had taken off my dressing gown and was lying next to her. I still couldn't quite believe that I was lying naked next to the girl I had always loved and that she was naked too. She was shaking slightly and she began to move her pelvis against my hand and we moved in rhythm together. All the time I was kissing her and, while she kissed me back, she began to gasp into my mouth. She opened her mouth wide against mine and began to moan loudly as she orgasmed. I was surprised that it had happened so quickly. When she had finished, I moved my face away from her's so that I could look at her properly. Her eyes were shut, her mouth was wide open and she was breathing quickly. She then turned towards me, opened her eyes and smiled again.

When Rosie's breathing returned to normal, I slid my left arm under the back of her neck and pulled her close to me. I kissed her gently on the lips before moving on top of her. She immediately spread her legs and I positioned myself between them. I was still in a state of disbelief that I was in bed with Rosie and that she was giving herself to me with such trust and passion. After I had finished, I lay still on top of Rosie for a while propping myself up slightly so as not to crush her. When my breathing returned to normal I rolled away from her and lay on my back. We lay side by side and held hands. It took me a little while to come down from what I could only describe as the most intense natural high I had ever experienced. A big smile spread across my face and without a word being spoken we turned towards each other, held each other and fell asleep.

# Chapter 8

*Monday*

I awoke on Monday morning to find that Rosie was not in the bed next to me. I turned to the alarm clock on the bedside table, hoping that it was before 7 a.m. when I knew that Mark was due to pick her up. I wanted to talk to my lovely girl, to hold her and to plan what we were going to do next. It was 8.30 a.m. and I had missed my chance. She had gone. If only she had woken me before she left I could have talked things through with her, or at least made a plan to talk or meet with her over the next couple of days. My mind was immediately filled with questions.

*Why hadn't she woken me before she left? Would she tell Mark what had happened before speaking to me? Should I call her today? Tomorrow? Would she call me? Should I go round to their house, on some pretext or another, to see her and hope he wasn't in?*

I needed a plan. I decided that I would leave it in Rosie's court for the rest of the day and, if I hadn't heard from her by lunchtime on Tuesday, I would risk calling her on her mobile. My plan made, I showered, dressed and left Butterfield Cottage. The long weekend was over and from an unpromising beginning, and for a reason I could never have imagined, I'd had the most fantastic time.

—

I arrived home early on Monday afternoon having checked my mobile countless times for a message from Rosie. Nothing. I desperately wanted to contact her but decided to stick to my plan. I unpacked and settled down in front of the TV to watch a film – any film – in the hope that it would take my mind off the situation I was in. At 5 p.m. I suddenly thought that I should have perhaps called Jilly to let her know I was back safely. She might be worried. Before I called her, two things went through my head. Firstly, if she had been at all worried then she would have called me, and secondly, would she somehow be able to tell from my voice that something was up? As soon as I asked myself the question, I knew the answer. She wouldn't be able to detect guilt in my voice because there wouldn't be any. I didn't feel guilty about what had happened at all. *She'd done it, why shouldn't I?*

At about 6 p.m. I decided to pop down to the local pub for a quick pint. Jilly was not due back until late the next evening and I wanted some company to take my mind off the events of the weekend. The Red Lion was one of those pubs which had managed to combine upmarket eating with a bar area that actually felt like a proper pub. Even Mark, who these days almost always ate and drank at the most exclusive places, loved to come in with Rosie, Jilly and I for the occasional Sunday lunch. I probably went to The Red Lion a couple of times a week and therefore knew quite a few of the locals. That meant that I could go there on my own and be pretty confident that there would be at least a couple of people I knew who would be happy to talk to me. I wanted normality after the weekend, and I was relieved to see Owen, Winkie and 'Billy the electrician' talking at the bar when I arrived.

'Billy the electrician' seemed pleased to see me. We only ever saw each other at the pub, but a joint love of football and the fact that he had helped Jilly and I with our malfunctioning wiring a couple of times, meant that we were very comfortable together. He was probably ten or twelve years younger than me, was a mad fan of Tottenham Hotspur Football Club and was a 'Mod'. Before Bradley Wiggins ever made it seem normal for a man in his early thirties to sport a mod haircut, Billy was doing it at The Red Lion. As a dyed-in-the-wool Spurs fan, Billy hated Arsenal and I, as an Arsenal fan, pretended to hate Spurs. We liked each other and got on very well.

"Hello Billy. How are you doing? Pint?"

"Fuck off, Arsenal. I wouldn't accept a drink from you— Oh alright then, I'll have a pint of lager."

I turned to Owen and Winkie and asked the same question, "Drink chaps?"

"Two pints of Guinness," bellowed Owen, in his broad Welsh accent.

Owen's accent was probably not that broad, as he had spent the last thirty years in London but it seemed, to my ears, as if he had just arrived from the Valleys. Owen was big, loud and charismatic. He ran and owned a communications company employing hundreds of people, but in the pub he was just a bloke who liked a beer and a laugh.

The final member of the group was Winkie. His real name was Rupert and none of us, including Winkie, knew where he had got his nickname. He was an 'Old Boy' of an ancient public school, in his mid-fifties. He had a pot belly, suspiciously dark-brown hair and dressed as if he had just come off a Scottish moor after a day's stalking. He was openly racist, sexist and homophobic. Rather incredibly, he was head of staff retention at a huge multi-national company. He obviously kept his views to himself when he was at work, although this was difficult to imagine bearing in mind that he was the most indiscreet man I had ever met.

After the first few gulps of my beer I had completely relaxed. The four of us rabbited on and on about sport, politics, women and bad behaviour. Owen, who was a mad rugby fan, told us a story about a recent incident on a rugby tour to Croatia. It involved a very drunk, naked man, a prostitute and a glass of antiseptic. The story was probably very funny, but, as usual, whenever Owen got to a funny bit he would dissolve into a fit of giggles, so you couldn't really tell. His giggles were infectious and, despite the fact that, because of his helpless laughter we couldn't really work out what was happening, we all laughed along heartily.

Two or three pints into the evening, I heard a huge commotion at the other end of the bar. I looked up and was shocked to see Mark charging across the pub towards me. I certainly hadn't expected to see him that night and definitely not under these circumstances. His face was twisted with rage and his fists were raised in front of his body and clenched tightly. Before I had time to react he had thrown himself at me. The shock and pain were enormous. His right hand connected flush on the side of my head and knocked me to the floor. As I lay on the ground, hands covering my face, Mark half lay on top of me and punched me hard in the stomach. My hands moved quickly from my face to protect my belly. Mark managed to sit on top of me and turned his attention to my head and face. His attack was frenzied and he must have hit me five times before Owen and Billy pulled him off. As they dragged him away he kicked out at me then stamped hard on my legs.

Bloodied and shocked, I tried to get to my feet but failed. It was all I could manage to sit up. Owen and Billy, strong men that they were, could barely restrain Mark. He was desperate to get to me and as they dragged him away I could hear him screaming, "You fucking scum! I'm gonna kill you, you bastard!"

He was still screaming at me when Owen and Billy finally managed to get him out of the pub. Even once they had got him outside, it was obvious they were having great difficulty preventing Mark from getting back inside. In the meantime, Winkie helped me to my feet and then on to a chair.

"Are you okay?"

"No, not really, I think my nose is broken."

There was a complete stunned silence from the rest of the pub.

"What the hell was that about?" continued Winkie who knew Mark from his occasional visits to the pub.

85

"Things took a strange turn at the weekend. He must be angry about it."

"What are you talking about? You and Mark are best mates. Hold on a minute, weren't you and Jilly with Mark and Rosie last weekend? What do you mean 'things took a strange turn'?"

"Not now, Winkie, I'm in pain."

I could still hear Mark screaming incomprehensibly outside the pub and could see, through the window in the entrance door, Owen and Billy standing with their backs to the door making sure he didn't get back in. Every now and again Mark would make another surge towards the pub door. These attempts to get back into the pub were, to my great relief, repulsed by Owen and Billy, who, like Winkie, knew Mark from his previous visits to The Red Lion.

"Calm down, Mark. Whatever it is, it's not worth it. Someone will call the police," shouted Owen. This seemed to have no effect on Mark who kept charging at the pub door. The landlord came over to Winkie and I, and put his hand on my shoulder.

"Look Tom, if you can manage it, why don't you and Winkie leave through the back door? That bloke is not calming down and you need to get out of here."

He led us through the bar-hatch and into a small room behind the bar. He unbolted the back door and gave us directions to get back on to the main road without going anywhere near the front entrance of the pub.

I obviously looked a complete mess because as soon as we were outside Winkie asked, "Do you want me to take you to hospital Tom?"

"No, I'm fine."

"Well at least come back to my place where we can get you cleaned up."

I was worried that Mark, if he ever stopped trying to smash his way back into the pub, would make his way to my house so I accepted Winkie's offer immediately

"Okay, thanks."

As we made our way back to his house I could hear police sirens in the distance. The sirens were obviously not for Mark, but I remember thinking that hopefully this would bring him to his senses and he would go home. However, I knew that Mark was not likely to give up easily on his mission to beat me half to death. Rosie had obviously told him what had happened at the Cottage the previous night and he was out for blood. He would undoubtedly try to hunt me down if he possibly could and that would definitely mean a trip to my house and maybe even a trip to the local hospital if he was thinking clearly enough. I was pretty sure he didn't know where Winkie lived, or even his real name, and that meant I would be safe there.

# Chapter 9

## *Tuesday in London*

Winkie's house turned out to be less than half a mile from the pub and just a few streets away from mine. The fact that I had, until the previous night, no idea where he, or indeed Owen or Billy, lived struck me as a bit strange. We had been good mates for at least ten years. I had spent time in their company at least once a week but, when I thought about it, I didn't actually know much about them. Billy's wife sometimes joined him at the pub and we were very friendly towards each other, but I didn't even know her name. Did Billy and his wife have kids? Where did they live? It was a similar situation with Owen. I knew what he did for a living, but I didn't really know much else.

We were a bunch of drinking mates who enjoyed each other's company but didn't really know much about each other's lives. We certainly didn't discuss our feelings let alone our emotions. Jilly, who had been to The Red Lion many times over the years, had asked me questions about my fellow drinkers to which I didn't know the answers. She said of my relationship with them, that the "depth of your superficiality amazes me." Despite all this, here I was waking up in Winkie's spare room. Neither he, Owen or Billy had hesitated to, firstly protect me, and secondly look after me when it really mattered. We might not know much about each other's lives outside the pub, but that didn't mean we weren't proper friends.

The first thing I felt when I woke up on Tuesday morning was physical pain. The whole of my face was throbbing and my ribs were aching so much that I could only take shallow breaths. For a moment I was completely disorientated and it took me a while to work out where I was. This was partly because Winkie's spare room was so different from how I pictured it would be. He had lived on his own since his divorce a couple of years earlier and I had imagined a shabby, badly decorated room with, perhaps, old photographs of his time at school, or in the army, adorning the walls. Well maybe the rest of the flat was like that, but waking up in his spare room was a bit like waking up in a hotel. The king size bed I had slept in was incredibly comfortable, with Egyptian cotton sheets and masses of duck-down pillows. The room was simply decorated with expensive looking furniture and beautiful paintings on the walls. The oil paintings were of landscapes, dogs and cows. They worked well in the bright and airy room and on closer inspection I was quite shocked to see Winkie's name written in the bottom left hand corner of each. He had never mentioned that he painted, or if he had, I hadn't been listening.

I got up slowly and left my bedroom to search for the bathroom. My head was thumping and every step I took was painful because of the bruising to my legs where Mark had stamped on them. On my search I stumbled across what must have been Winkie's room. It too was tastefully decorated and had a beautiful *en suite* bathroom. I continued my search, passing a third bedroom before finding what I was looking for. I had no time to be impressed by more tasteful décor because immediately, as I entered the room, I was confronted by my reflection in the mirror above the sink. The image staring back at me was barely recognisable. My whole face was swollen and covered in dried blood. My right eye was almost entirely closed and I could see the beginnings of yellow and purple bruising both above and below what was essentially just a narrow slit. I was amazed I could see quite so well out of it.

My concern for myself was, however, pretty minimal. I was more concerned about what to say to Jilly and when I should say it. I couldn't risk Mark speaking to her first and giving his version of events. I knew I had to call her immediately. Making that call was not easy. I decided not to even attempt to explain anything over the phone. Instead, I tried to get her to agree to meet me for lunch. She had told me before she left Wiltshire that she was going to have an incredibly busy couple of days, so I knew she would be reluctant to agree to meet me. I took a deep breath and tapped in her number. Thankfully, she answered almost immediately.

"Hello."

"Hi, Jilly it's me."

"Hi."

"How are things going?"

"I'm really busy. I can't chat for long I've got lots to do. What's wrong?"

"Can we meet for lunch?"

"Tom, I've just told you I'm busy, I haven't got time."

"There's something I need to discuss with you urgently and it can't be done over the phone."

"Is it the kids? Are they ok?"

"They're fine. It's got nothing to do with the kids and nobody's ill, I just need to meet up. Urgently."

"What is it? Can't this wait until tonight?"

"I told you, Jilly. I need to talk face to face and no, it can't wait until tomorrow."

"Alright, alright. Meet me at Carlucci's just around the corner from the office. I'll be there at 12.30 but I can only stay for half an hour. This better be good."

"Thanks, Jilly, I'll see you at 12.30."

Jilly had been her usual abrupt self, but I'd expected that. The important thing was that she'd agreed to meet. By far the more difficult conversation was still to come and I didn't know at this stage what on earth I was going to say.

Winkie was in the kitchen when I came down the stairs. He was frying bacon and sipping a large mug of tea.

He greeted me with, "Fuck me, you look dreadful. Bacon sarnie?"

The bacon looked too good to refuse and I still had more than four hours before I was due to meet Jilly. I decided that I would enjoy Winkie's hospitality and only when I got home would I give proper thought to exactly what I would say to Jilly.

"What the fuck was last night about?" Winkie asked, "What was up with Mark?" I didn't want to discuss the previous night or the weekend with Winkie.

"It's complicated," I said, evasively. "I'll talk to you about it when I've sorted things out."

Winkie could tell that he would get no more out of me, so he didn't ask me anything else.

It only took me about twenty minutes to get home and, considering I was unable to move at anything other than a snail's pace, it struck me again just how close to each other Winkie and I lived. When I arrived I went straight upstairs to the bathroom. A long soak in the bath and a good think about exactly what I would say to Jilly was what I needed. A glance in the bathroom mirror confirmed my resemblance to a particularly untalented boxer who had just taken a terrible beating. There was less evidence on show of the pounding my ribs had taken, just a little bit of redness, but the pain every time I breathed in was excruciating.

I lay full length in the bath with a cold flannel over my face and thought about how I would approach my lunchtime conversation with Jilly. I needed to get to the point as soon as possible. Not only had I committed adultery, but I had done it with one of her best friends. I would explain that we had got a bit drunk on Sunday evening and that one thing led to another and we ended up in bed. Even as I was rehearsing the words in my head, I knew that they were inadequate and blunt to the point of insulting, but I couldn't think of a better way to do it.

By the time the doorbell rang I had got out of the bath, dressed and was in the kitchen having a cigarette. My first thought was that maybe it was Mark and that I was in no condition to face another onslaught from him. I went to the living room and peered out of the window to see if I could catch a glimpse of who was at the door. I knew that this was impossible unless they had rung the bell and then taken several steps backwards, but it did give me time to come to the conclusion that it was very unlikely to be Mark. Unless he'd become a completely different person overnight, there was no way that he would have done anything other than hammer loudly and relentlessly on the door. I knew him, and he would not have been able to calm himself until he had properly exacted revenge. I opened the door and there in front of me stood two men in their late twenties or early thirties. Before I had a chance to speak, they introduced themselves as Detective Sergeant Sean Lane and Detective Constable Chris McLean. My first thought was there had been some sort of complaint made about Mark's behaviour the previous evening. The last thing I wanted was for this whole mess to be further complicated by some busybody making a complaint to the police.

"Good morning sir, can you confirm that you are—"

"Listen, guys, I'm fine," I interrupted, "What happened in the pub was essentially just a disagreement between friends. I've got no intention of pressing charges."

Detective Sergeant Lane opened his mouth to speak again but once more I interrupted him.

"I really am fine. No bones broken. No harm done."

Finally, in a raised voice, he managed to ask his question, "Are you Mr Tom Bishop?"

"This is not necessary. I'm perfectly fine and I don't wish to either make a complaint or take the matter any further."

*"Are you Mr Tom Bishop?"*

"Yes, I am, but I've got no intention of making a fuss about what was just a bit of an argument between friends in the pub."

"We're not here to talk about an incident in a pub, Mr Bishop. We are here to tell you that you are under arrest on suspicion of rape. You do not have to say anything, but it may harm your defence if you do not mention, when questioned, something which you later rely on in court. Anything you *do* say may be given in evidence."

I don't remember whether I said anything else at this stage, but I do remember feeling sick and literally going weak at the knees. The policemen led me away to their car. I think they put me in handcuffs before leading me away. Sitting in the police car did little to help me think clearly. The shock of what had happened left me physically weak and mentally paralysed. I sat in complete silence for quite some time before I regained some sort of composure and began to piece together, in my shattered mind, what had just happened. Mark had obviously been told by Rosie that we had made love at the Cottage. Why she would have told him I don't know. She could've at least spoken to me first. Mark must have been raging when she told him and bullied her into claiming that she had been forced to have sex with me. At that stage, this seemed to me the only way of explaining what was happening. Not only had a beautiful moment in my life been ruined, but Mark was trying to ruin my whole life. I knew that if he found out what had happened he would want revenge, but I never imagined how far he would go to reap that revenge.

# Chapter 10

## *Under arrest*

The policemen didn't speak to each other, or to me, for the first twenty minutes of our journey and I was in too much of a stunned state to ask them any questions. It was only once I realised that we were heading west and out of London that I finally engaged them in conversation. I was confused as to where they were taking me. I had assumed that I would be taken to the nearest police station. When I asked them where we were going, I was told that, as the alleged crime had taken place on their 'patch', they were taking me to Overbury Police Station in Wiltshire. I was given this information by Detective Sergeant Lane who had first spoken to me on my doorstep and I noticed for the first time that he had a thick West Country accent. That was the only time that I spoke during the two and a half hour journey.

When we arrived at the police station, I was led to the front desk where I was booked in by the custody officer. He was matter-of-fact and smiling. If he knew what I had been arrested for, he was not letting it affect his cheerful approach to his job. I, on the other hand, was feeling desperate. Amongst other things, he explained to me that I was entitled to free legal advice and to a phone call. I listened as well as I could to what he had to say and decided that because I hadn't done anything wrong I didn't need legal advice, but that I definitely needed to contact Jilly to tell her where I was. In my confused state I decided not to tell her that I had been arrested. I was still hoping, for no good reason, that the police would realise their mistake and just let me go.

I had to use a landline to call Jilly as all my possessions, including my mobile phone, had been taken away from me. I rang her mobile and hoped that she would pick up, even though she obviously wouldn't recognise the number. The phone rang for what seemed like an eternity, but eventually she answered.

"Jilly Bishop," she said in her most professional voice.

"Hi, it's me."

"Hi."

"Listen, I'm sorry to mess you around but I'm not going to make lunch. I've had to go—"

"Oh for Christ's sake. I've had to rearrange my day around lunch with you and now you cancel at the last minute."

"Jilly, I'm sorry, but it's unavoidable, I'm at the—"

"What on earth can you be doing that's so important?" she interrupted me again.

Her dismissive attitude riled me and I was very tempted just to blurt out the truth, but I managed to contain myself.

"There was a fight at the pub last night and the police want me to give them a witness statement. I'm at the police station at the moment. I'll probably be here for a few hours."

There was a pause at the other end of the line and, for a split second, I thought she might be concerned about me, or at least interested. This was the one time that I didn't want her to be interested in what was going on in my life. True to form – she wasn't.

"Well, I'm going to be very late tonight so don't worry about dinner. I'll probably grab something to eat at the office. Don't wait up. Bye."

I think she had already hung up by the time I said goodbye.

For once, I was relieved about Jilly's indifference to what was going on in my life and pleased that she was going to be home very late. My conversation with her had somehow brought me to my senses and, as I was led away from the front desk, I understood that the police were not going to realise their mistake and that my ordeal was just beginning. I was told that I would be kept in a cell until they were ready to question me, and it became obvious to me that I would not be going anywhere for some time. The thought crossed my mind that Jilly might even be home before me.

As I sat on the bed in my cell, I looked down to see that the laces had been removed from my shoes. It was this sight that fully brought home to me the horror of my situation. For one of the few times in my adult life I thought I was going to cry. I fought this impulse very hard. Having been brought up by a strict father who was dismissive of any show of emotion by a man, I tended to shut down when faced with circumstances that were likely to lead to tears. The last time I had cried was when I was about twelve and my father hadn't just been dismissive he'd actually been very angry. I forced myself to think, as clearly as possible, about what was happening to me and what I should do. I hadn't done anything wrong, but I knew that didn't mean I wasn't in a whole world of trouble.

I started to question the wisdom of refusing the opportunity to call a lawyer when given the chance and wondered whether I should ask for one before answering any questions. I decided that, lawyer or no lawyer, I would just tell the police exactly what happened. This was not the time to think about denying adultery for the sake of my marriage to Jilly. I was going to tell the police that I had consensual sex with Rosie and then, when I got home, I was going to tell Jilly the same thing. I felt physically sick at the prospect of both of these conversations but, if anything, the interview with the police would be more straightforward. I would go over the story in my mind and just give an exact account. The conversation with Jilly would be much more difficult.

The cell was in the basement of the police station. There was no natural light due to the absence of a window and everything inside the cell was either grey or brown. All four walls, the ceiling and floor were grey. The single bed had a grey frame, light grey sheets and a dark grey pillow. For a bit of colour, the blanket was brown. As I paced up and down, feelings of frustration and then anger began to rise within me. I couldn't believe I was in this situation. For the first time since I had started going out with Jilly, I had been unfaithful, and now I was accused of rape. Mark had been constantly unfaithful to Rosie both before and during their marriage and he had just got away with it. He had even been admired in certain quarters. I was frustrated that I had made one mistake and my world had fallen apart. He seemed to win out every time and the one time he had lost to me, he was obviously determined to make sure that I lost more. I was angry that my marriage and liberty could be taken away from me just because he couldn't bear to lose.

Anger and frustration were soon replaced by the now familiar feeling of panic as a series of questions raced through my mind.

*How long would I be in this cell? Having initially declined the opportunity would I even get the chance to speak to a solicitor before the police questioned me? When would they question me? Surely they wouldn't charge me on the basis of Rosie's word against mine? If they did, would they keep me in jail until the trial? When would that be?*

I could feel the tears welling up in my eyes, but I refused to give in and start sobbing. I took some deep breaths and tried to think clearly. I knew that I needed to get my story straight and that I had to un-jumble my thoughts regarding the events of Sunday. I replayed over and over in my mind, not just how Rosie and I had spent the day, but exactly which parts of the day the staff at the Cottage had witnessed. I was certain that the police would jump on any inconsistency or inaccuracy during the interview and I was determined to make sure that didn't happen. Obviously, the part on which I concentrated most was the time I had spent in Rosie's bedroom. I made sure that I not only went over the facts, but also the emotions that I had felt.

Once I was confident that I knew exactly what I was going to say, the stupidity of electing not to have legal representation struck me. When I had been asked if I wanted to contact a solicitor I had refused because in my mind saying "yes" would have been an admission of guilt. I decided that, even if my change of mind irritated the police, I was definitely going to get a solicitor involved. I felt much calmer once this decision was made and determined that I would try and think about something else for the rest of the time I was in my cell. My mind went back to the only other time I had found myself in a cell. I forced myself to think back to, what now seemed like, a much happier and less complicated time.

—

I was twenty-one years old and had been working for a few months as a trainee salesman at a company that sold photocopiers. Pete, one of the older guys in the sales team, was getting married and he invited a number of us to his stag night. The whole evening was a bit of an eye-opener for someone fresh out of university. In my naivety, I had thought that I was a man of the world who'd already experienced pretty much the full array of laddish behaviour. I was wrong – very wrong.

Pete was a good-looking man in his late twenties whose reputation was that of something of a 'player'.

Rumour had it that he'd bedded quite a few of the girls in the office. This, along with a sharp wit and, what seemed to me at the time to be, effortless charm, meant that he was a bit of a hero to me and the other younger members of the sales team. I was surprised to hear that he was getting married because he seemed to be the archetypal womaniser. The woman he was marrying was apparently his long-term girlfriend. I was quite shocked when he told me this, but his obvious infidelity didn't concern me too much. That was his business, and I was just looking forward to the stag night.

I don't know what I was expecting – perhaps a few beers and a couple of strippers – but it was far more extreme than anything I could have imagined. The evening began in a pub close to the office. The drinking was ferocious. Several pints with double chasers were required to be drunk in the hour or so spent in that first pub. I was very drunk, therefore, before we even arrived at the main stag night venue, which was another pub near the Albert Bridge in Chelsea. We were greeted by the Irish landlord who shepherded us upstairs to the function room. There we were met by a grotesquely fat and sweaty looking man who turned out to be the evening's comedian.

If there was anything more grotesque than the physical appearance of the comedian, it was the stream of racist, homophobic and sexist jokes that followed one after the other. However, I can't say I was shocked. It was the mid 1980's and that sort of thing was still pretty commonplace. I was so drunk by the time he'd finished his set that very few things could have shocked me. One of the things that *could* have shocked me – then happened. Two strippers appeared from a side door and took centre stage. Even in my, by now, totally inebriated state I recognised that they were quite old, quite fat and quite aggressive. They wasted no time in stripping Pete completely naked and attaching a dog collar and lead around his neck. They then took it in turns, after forcing him onto all-fours, to ride him around the stage hitting him hard and often with a riding crop that they shared. He was so drunk that he barely seemed to notice. They then sat him in a chair and tied a piece of string around one of his big toes. I remember wondering why on earth they had done such a thing, until they tied the other end around his penis. The string was just too short to allow Pete to stand up without one, if not both, of his appendages being yanked hard.

The strippers then began their striptease in front of Pete. They didn't just strip. Every thirty seconds or so they would call him out of his chair to join them. He would rise unsteadily from his chair, be pulled up short by the piece of string and collapse to the floor in agony. The strippers would then help him back on to the chair and begin the process again. Pete was so drunk that by the next time they called him over to join them, he seemed to have totally forgotten about the string. The whole scene was fascinating, horrifying and hilarious all at the same time.

After torturing Pete for quite a while, the strippers then announced that they would be retiring to two small rooms just off the function room, and they would be more than happy to welcome "paying guests." From nowhere, the Irish landlord appeared and said that he was "going first", adding that he would be grateful if somebody could keep an eye out for his wife in case she left the bar downstairs to come looking for him. I remember looking on at this scene in disbelief. Surely the landlord wasn't going to screw one of the strippers while his wife was serving downstairs in the bar? As it turned out – yes he was. Not only that, but at least half of the stag party then formed two orderly queues and patiently waited their turn to visit one or other of the strippers. Pete actually queued up twice. I'm pretty sure he didn't know what he was queuing up for and even more sure that he was incapable of getting his money's worth.

When the stag night broke up, I'd actually received a bit of 'stick' for not joining in fully. It was this, and the fact that I was very drunk, that led to me being arrested and locked up in a cell for the first time. Along with Ewan, who had joined the sales force with me, I concocted a plan to prove to my fellow stags that I was just as much of a man as the rest of them. Close to the pub was a major junction controlled by traffic lights. Once the lights had turned red, Ewan was to run across the road, with me apparently in hot pursuit. I would catch up with him in the middle of the road and wrestle him to the ground. We would then simulate a fight in front of queuing traffic. This was all to be watched by the remnants of the stag party and would, in my eyes, prove to them that I was no wimp. It was a pretty stupid plan and it went badly wrong.

Along with a few shocked onlookers sitting in their cars at the traffic lights, was a police van. While Ewan and I were concentrating on carrying out our simulated brawl, four Met policeman jumped out of the van, ran towards us and started pulling us apart. The two of us were dragged off to the van and thrown inside. We were ordered to place our hands on the bar running across the bench seat in front of us. Each time I took my hands off the bar in order to explain the innocence of our actions, I was forcibly made to put them back by an angry looking policeman who didn't seem to find my explanation in any way amusing. The third time I raised my hands he grabbed me in a headlock, pushed me up against a window and ordered one of his colleagues to cuff me.

As far as I could remember, when we arrived at the police station, very little was said to us before we were bodily thrown into separate cells. The difference between my first stint in a police cell and my second, twenty-five years later, was that during the first episode I was too drunk to care and was pretty confident that nothing too serious was going to happen to me. I was proven right and although we were kept overnight in the cells, no charges were brought against us and they sent us on our way early the next morning.

—

The situation I now found myself in, more than two decades later, was much more serious and there was no drunkenness to even numb the fear. My fond memories of those simpler times were quickly replaced with a, now familiar, feeling of dread. I still couldn't believe what was happening to me. Just as I thought I couldn't cope anymore, I heard footsteps in the corridor outside my cell and the sound of keys unlocking the door. The sense of relief was almost overwhelming as I saw the unsmiling face of a young, uniformed police officer appear to tell me that they were ready to interview me. I had probably been in the cell less than half an hour, but it felt like an eternity.

As the young policeman lead me along the corridor, I told him that I had changed my mind about wanting legal advice. He explained to me that he wasn't the person to speak to and that I needed to tell the interviewing officers when I got to the interview room. He seemed completely disinterested in whether I wanted a solicitor or not. His job was merely to escort me to the appropriate place. When I arrived in the interview room I was greeted by Detectives Lane and McLean. My request for a solicitor seemed to make no difference to them either. It struck me that, while I had been going through hell for the last few hours, the rest of the world had just carried on with business as usual.

# Chapter 11

## *Interview*

The police didn't allow me to make a call directly from my mobile phone to a solicitor. Under their supervision, I was allowed to retrieve the number I wanted from my contacts, write it down and then call from a landline in the station. The solicitor I called was an old friend of mine who I'd become reacquainted with over the last few years. Charles Burton had been at university with me where he studied law. He had gone on to train as a solicitor and had practiced as a defence lawyer for over twenty years.

We had been great mates at university and for five or so years after we left. In our late twenties, we drifted apart and had only met up by chance a couple of years earlier at a rugby club dinner. We were the pre-email, pre-text and pre-social media generation, and when our lives had gone in different directions we had lost touch. But from the moment we bumped into each other again, it was as if the previous fifteen years of separation hadn't happened. We were, if anything, closer than we had ever been.

Charles had acted as the defence solicitor in some of the most high profile cases of recent years. He had defended armed robbers, suspected terrorists and an array of violent criminals. The call I made to him from Overbury Police Station had begun formally enough because he had not recognised the number from which I was calling, but had then descended into farce and had finally become stutteringly serious. The conversation had descended into farce, because as soon as Charles realised that it was me on the line he had launched into his best Rab C Nesbitt/Billy Connolly impersonation. The reason for this was historical. In our college days we had discovered that we enjoyed trying out accents on each other. Our favourite was a guttural, barely understandable, Glaswegian shipyard's accent. Now, in our mid-forties, we almost always began any telephone conversation in, what was probably a pretty inaccurate, Glaswegian accent. Before he realised who he was talking to, Charles had started off quite normally.

"Charles Burton"

"Hi Charles, it's Tom. I've got a bit of a problem—"

As soon as he realised who it was, he interrupted me and started bellowing, "AWREET BIG YIN. HOW AR YE, YE FREAK. YAFFA YAT? WHIT YAT YAFFER?" (Hello big man. How are you, you strange man. Are you off a yacht? Which yacht are you off of?)

"Charles I've got a problem—"

"KEEP YUR HEED AND I'LL BUY YE A BUNNET." (Keep your head and I'll buy you a hat.)

He then began singing, "SLEETER SLATTER HOLY WAATER—"

"Charles, I need to talk to you—"

"IT'SA BRAW BRICHT MOONLICHT NICHT THE NICHT, I'M AWFY PISHED YE NUMPTY" (It's a beautiful bright moonlit night tonight. I'm awfully drunk, you idiot.)

Charles was making such a racket at the other end of the phone that he was easily audible to the police officers who were monitoring the call. Out of the corner of my eye I could see them stifling their laughter. I raised my voice in an attempt to stop him.

"STOP! CHARLES, I'M IN TROUBLE."

Finally he lowered his voice, "What?"

"I've got a big problem and I need your help."

"What is it?

When I told Charles that I'd been arrested on suspicion of rape, he didn't seem to understand.

"What do you mean?"

"I mean that I've been arrested on suspicion of rape and I need your help?"

There was a long pause. Charles had certainly been confronted with this type of thing, and worse, in the past, but he seemed lost for words. The difference this time was that he was dealing with a friend. Eventually he spoke.

"Where? Where are you, Tom?"

"I'm at Overbury Police Station in Wiltshire and I have just exercised my right to legal advice. Can you get here as soon as possible?"

There was another long pause before Charles spoke again. He seemed very distracted.

"Of course. Of course. Who are you supposed to have raped, Tom?"

Then, suddenly, before I could answer, Charles' tone changed completely, "Don't answer that question, Tom. I will be there in about two hours, maybe sooner depending upon the traffic. Please don't say anything to anybody until you have spoken to me. Try to stay calm and remember – don't say anything."

As soon as I put down the telephone I was ushered back to the cells. On the way downstairs, I felt my panic rising again. I found it hard to breathe. I did not want to be confined in that cell again. I'd never suffered from claustrophobia or an irrational fear in my life, but irrational and afraid is the only way I could describe how I was feeling. I gritted my teeth and started talking to myself inwardly.

*Come on, get a grip. I'll only be in that cell for another couple of hours and then Charles will be here. Toughen up. Be a man.*

It seemed to do the trick. I felt the fear subsiding and my breathing return to normal. Inside the cell, I sat down on the bed and waited.

I didn't have my mobile or my watch so I couldn't be sure, but it was probably nearly three hours before I heard the, by now familiar, sound of footsteps approaching my cell. The door was unlocked and I was told to "Follow me" by the same young, uniformed officer. As I walked along the corridor familiar thoughts raced around my head.

*What's going to happen to me? Are they going to prosecute me? Surely not. It's a case of her word against mine. When am I going to get out of this dreadful place? Today? Tomorrow? Will there be a trial? Will I be given bail? How the fuck am I going to explain this to Jilly?*

I was in quite a state by the time I reached the interview room. The door was opened by the escorting police officer and there, to my almost overwhelming relief, sat Charles. The interview room was very similar to my cell. Grey floors, ceilings and walls, brown plastic chairs and a grey table. The one feature of the room that differed markedly from my cell was the window. Although the glass in the window was heavily frosted, the natural light that flooded into the room lifted my spirits. The door was closed behind me and we were left alone. Charles got to his feet and moved towards me. I reached out to shake his hand, which he bypassed in order to give me a hug.

I stepped back from Charles and looked at him. He was wearing a stylishly cut, charcoal grey, three-piece suit, a crisp, white shirt and a dark red tie. It was strange to see him in a suit, as in his everyday life he shunned any sort of formality. His normal dress was baggy jeans, DM's and a dark T-shirt. He was, I suppose, a bit 'trendy' with an emphasis on the casual. Unlike so many others in their forties who try to look cool and end up looking a bit sad, Charles actually did come across as pretty cool. He was helped in this regard by having a completely bald head. While his premature balding had distressed him a great deal in his early and mid-twenties, he had taken the plunge and shaving off his remaining hair at an early age had worked well for him.

"Hi Tom, how are you?" he asked.

"Not great really" I replied, desperately trying to keep any emotion out of my voice.

Before he could say anything else I told him that I hadn't done anything wrong. I was keen that he knew this from the outset, not just as my lawyer but, more importantly, as my friend. I told him that I didn't know why any of this was happening to me. At this point Charles took control of meeting. He explained that while he was pleased, on a personal level, that I was adamant about my innocence, the best way to proceed was for him to deal with me as if he didn't know me. He stressed that he needed to divorce the personal from the professional. I was relieved that he had taken control.

He told me that he had spent some time speaking to the arresting officers, prior to talking to me, and that he wanted to make sure that I clearly understood what I had been arrested for. He also told me that he knew why my face was in such a mess. Having done this he then asked me to recount exactly what had happened between me and Rosie. I told him about the weekend. I told him about Mark's boorish behaviour and I told him about Jilly and Mark leaving early on Sunday morning. I then described the time that Rosie and I had spent together. Charles was, for obvious reasons, particularly interested in this. He asked me to go into as much detail as possible as to what Rosie and I had spoken about, where we had specifically been during the day and whether anybody else had either seen us together or overheard anything we discussed.

"Was anyone else, other than you and Rosie, in the breakfast room on Sunday morning?"

I struggled to remember, mostly because I was so preoccupied with being alone with Rosie, but eventually recalled that there was one lady who came into the dining room a couple of times during breakfast, to clear plates and make sure we had everything we needed.

"Would she have heard the two of you planning your activities for the day?" he asked.

"Well actually, Charles, I do remember that after we had discussed our plan for the day, Rosie was quite excited and listed everything we were going to do. I think the lady was standing in the corner of the room while Rosie did this."

"Do you think the lady was listening? Could she have heard Rosie?"

"She definitely *could* have heard her, but I don't know whether she was listening or not."

Charles continued asking questions specifically about whether there were any other witnesses to the intimate day that Rosie and I had spent together. I told him that there was definitely no one else there when we went swimming, but on our walk up to the lodge by the lake we had seen a couple of the younger members of staff. They would definitely have seen us laughing and joking. I also remembered that one of the girls who had seen us walking up to the lodge had later come in and helped Rosie lay out lunch. This girl might also have seen that Rosie was wearing different clothes from those she'd been wearing on the walk.

And then, I remembered. That afternoon, as we watched the film, Rosie had been draped all over me. I recalled that the same girl that had helped lay out lunch had seen us lying on the sofa together. She would probably have known that we were not a couple and may have thought that our intimacy was a little inappropriate. I told Charles that the only other person we had seen for the rest of the day was the cook. We had enjoyed, what could only be described as, an intimate evening alone together, but no one else, to my knowledge, had seen us. I described how we had reminisced, shared a cigarette and finally how when we had finished our cigarette she had led me by the arm back into the house.

"What happened next?" asked Charles.

I recognised that my exact recollection of what had happened after Rosie and I had finished dinner was absolutely vital. I tried to recall every single detail from the moment I had entered Rosie's bedroom. I was embarrassed to be discussing this with Charles initially, but the dispassionate way in which he asked the most intimate questions somehow made things easier. I told him that I had quietly knocked on her bedroom door and then walked in without waiting for a response. I explained that she had said nothing as I stood motionless at the end of her bed. I went on to say that I saw her lack of communication as a sign that she was happy that I was there. I stressed the fact that she did not recoil from me either when I sat on the bed or when I first reached out, touched her face and gently pushed her back onto the bed.

Charles interrupted my description of the events to ask more specific questions, "I take it from what you've said so far that you did not at anytime ask Rosie if it was okay to be in the room or sitting on the bed?"

"No. I didn't."

"Before you laid hands on her, did you say anything?"

"No."

"Did she say anything?"

"No."

"Before you moved her from the sitting position to lying down on the bed did either of you say anything?"

"No."

As I answered Charles' questions, I began to think that perhaps my situation wasn't looking very good and I said as much to him. In my panic, I even suggested that perhaps it would be better if I said that I did ask Rosie's consent and that she had given it. Charles reacted quickly and decisively to my suggestion, explaining that I had nothing at all to hide and that I should just tell the truth. I wasn't convinced initially because it sounded quite bad to me that at no point had I asked for Rosie's consent and at no point had she said anything that could be construed as giving it. Charles reassured me that this was not necessarily a problem and although it would be better if she had said something, that it was clear from my description that the situation had developed gradually and that there had been 'implied consent'. He explained that if things did ever get to the stage of an actual trial that the concept of 'implied consent' would be vital to my defence.

Despite my, in retrospect, idiotic protestations, Charles then insisted that I described the sex that followed in as much detail as possible. He frequently interrupted my description to ask whether we had indulged in any unusual sexual practices.

"Did you at any time use enough force to have left cuts or bruising or any other type of marks?"

"No, of course not," I replied.

"Are you sure? When you pushed Rosie back onto the bed you said that you put your hands around her neck? Could you have left any bruising?" he persisted.

"No, no – I didn't put my hands around her neck. I put one hand up to her neck and guided her backwards. There is no chance I could have left any bruising. I didn't use any pressure, I just guided her backwards."

"Did she resist in any way?"

"No, she just lay down."

Charles's questions were all very clinical and, after a while, I realised that this was absolutely the necessary approach. He asked his questions in a completely unemotional way, and, although I found this disconcerting at first, after a while I was able to answer them in an equally unemotional way.

"No, I didn't bite her at any time or suck any part of her body in a way that would have left any marks."

"I did not slap any part of her body or face."

"I am sure that there would have been no bruising on the inside of her thighs or anywhere else on her legs."

I was just about getting used to the fact that it was obviously necessary for Charles to ask these questions, when he took the questioning to a different level, a level that made me feel very uncomfortable.

"Did you at any time insert your fingers into her anus?"

"Did you insert your penis into her anus?"

When I objected to the intimacy or the nature of the questions being asked, Charles slapped me down quickly and hard.

"Listen Tom, you need to just answer the questions. I have to know exactly what did and didn't happen. You can be absolutely certain that if you fail to tell the police anything that they consider important now, it will cause you big problems in the future. Rosie will almost certainly have had a full medical examination and if there are any marks on her that are not explained by what you say, then it won't look good."

"Okay. Okay, I understand."

When Charles had finished questioning me, I asked him what was going to happen next. He explained that I would now be interviewed by the police under caution and that I should tell them exactly what I had told him. He further explained that bearing in mind that the sex I had with Rosie was completely consensual, I had nothing at all to hide and that therefore I should just tell them everything. It was probably a straightforward situation for Charles in terms of him not having to coach me on any answers I was going to give, but I was desperately nervous about the whole situation. I was particularly anxious about what would happen after the interview. The big question in my mind was whether I would be remanded in custody. I couldn't stand the thought of spending any more time in that dingy cell. Charles explained to me that there was a chance that the police would not grant me bail and that after the interview I would remain in custody. This terrified me.

The thought of spending weeks or, for all I knew, months in prison awaiting trial for something that I hadn't done sent me into a panic once more. I could literally feel the bile rising inside of me and was doing all I could to stop myself from throwing up. I was also embarrassed to be reacting in this way in front of Charles. I'd always tried to present myself, to my male friends at least, as the sort of man who could cope with anything, and here I was about to throw up. I managed to contain myself, just long enough to hear Charles tell me that although it was possible that I would not get police bail, it was highly unlikely. I knew that he wasn't just saying this to calm me down and slowly my panic subsided.

After Charles had asked all the questions he needed to and briefed me on what to expect from the police, I was taken back to my cell. I didn't have to spend long there, before I was taken back to the interview room where I was reunited with Charles. We sat opposite Detectives Lane and McLean across a small grey table, which had recording equipment at one end. I felt strangely calm and for the first time since I had been arrested on my doorstep, I took a good look at the two police officers opposite me. To say they looked unthreatening was an understatement. Lane, the older of the two, wore a tweed sports jacket over a pale blue shirt, tan coloured jeans and brogues. He looked like an off-duty army officer. McLean was less smartly dressed in jeans and a red T-shirt and could have passed for one of my elder son's school friends.

Their approach to questioning me was as unthreatening as they looked. I had expected a good cop/bad cop routine, but I only got politeness from both of them. Sergeant Lane concentrated specifically on what had happened from the moment I had entered Rosie's bedroom to the time that we started to have intercourse. He claimed that Rosie had asked me what I was doing in her room and then what I was doing sitting on her bed. Obviously, I denied that any such questions had been asked or indeed that there had been any communication between us during the whole episode. I managed to stay calm throughout the whole process, although it was difficult when they put it to me that when I first reached out to touch Rosie, she had pushed my hand away and recoiled. It was more difficult still to remain calm when they suggested that I had responded to Rosie pushing my hand away by forcing her backwards so that she was lying flat on the bed and then had held her down, while I raped her. They accused me of putting my hand over her mouth when she said "Please, Tom. Stop."

# Chapter 12

## *Waiting*

After the interview was over, I was returned to my cell where I had time to both think and fret. I was pleased with how the interview had gone. I had been given the chance to describe the lovely day that Rosie and I had spent together and, at the suggestion of Charles, had strongly emphasised the intimacy of the day. I also felt that I had kept my cool when I was challenged over exactly what had happened after I entered her bedroom. After having given due consideration to the good and bad parts of the interview, my mind quickly turned to what was going to happen next. The thought of not being granted bail, however unlikely, and spending any more time in my cell, was still at the front of my mind. I was also thinking about the best way to break the news of my awful predicament to Jilly. I decided that if I didn't get bail then I was going to ask Charles to go and see her. If I was released? Well, I would think about that if, and when, it happened.

I didn't have to wait long. It couldn't have been more than twenty minutes before I heard those, by now familiar, footsteps approaching my cell. The door was unlocked and I was taken back upstairs. On the way up the stairs I was told that I was to be bailed to return to the police station at a future date. The relief was very much a physical experience. It was as if I could finally exhale and breathe in fresh air. I felt my legs buckle slightly and I reached out to steady myself. I still had the daunting prospect of telling Jilly what had happened and the even more daunting prospect of possibly being charged with rape, but at least , for the moment, I was out of that cell.

The whole process of being bailed passed me by as a bit of a blur, but the end result was that I was to return to the police station in four weeks time. After signing a couple of forms I found myself outside with Charles. For some reason I expected it to be dark and miserable when I finally emerged from the station, but it was the most beautiful, sunny autumn evening. I hugged Charles with relief and then started to quiz him on what I could expect to happen next. He explained to me, in hushed tones, that when I returned to the police station I would either be charged with a crime, almost certainly rape, or that I would not be charged with anything. He further explained that the police might want to interview some of the staff at the Cottage to see if any of them had anything relevant to say, and that they would then need to send my file off to the Crown Prosecution Service. Charles told me that it would be the CPS who would decide whether I would be charged or not.

I started to ask Charles more questions, but he stopped me in my tracks by saying that perhaps right outside the police station was not the best place for us to be discussing things. He suggested that we go and find a pub where we could sit in a quiet corner and not be disturbed. The first one we came to was no more than a couple of hundred yards away and was typical of many you find in market towns across the country. Too many hanging baskets, overflowing with improbably coloured flowers, dominated the front of the pub. There was a small outside seating area, which one lonely, late-afternoon drinker inhabited. As we walked through the door of The Queens Head I glanced at my watch. I was surprised to see that it was only 6.15 p.m. It felt like several days ago that the police had come knocking at my door.

The wooden floorboards creaked underfoot as we approached the bar. We stood silently as I ordered two orange juices. I would have loved a beer, but I needed a clear head so that I could fully concentrate on making sure I asked all the questions which were racing around my brain. We settled into a corner of the pub.

"How will the CPS make their decision?' I asked, immediately.

"Well, they'll look at two things. Firstly, whether it is in the public interest to prosecute and secondly, whether there is a reasonable prospect of gaining a conviction."

I paused for a few seconds while I considered what Charles was telling me. I remember thinking that the terminology that he used was familiar to me. This was not because of any direct experience of police procedure, but because I had read or heard these phrases in either the newspapers or on television. I never imagined that I would have to apply them to myself.

"Right… I can see that it would be in the public interest to prosecute someone for rape, but surely there is not enough evidence to prosecute me for it? It's her word against mine," I said hopefully.

Charles looked straight at me and grimaced.

"Look, until fairly recently Rosie's evidence on it's own would not be enough for the CPS to decide to prosecute, but things have changed. I have to be honest with you, these days it's likely that they will decide to prosecute."

I felt like I had been kicked in the stomach. It seemed ridiculous to me that you could be accused by someone of raping them and even though there were no witnesses and no signs of force being used, you would probably be prosecuted and end up in court.

I made my thoughts clear to Charles.

"This is ludicrous, I haven't done anything wrong. Just because that bastard has forced Rosie to accuse me of rape, me and my whole family are going to go through hell. Surely there's no chance I'll be found guilty? Please tell me that."

My fear had turned to anger and then back to fear and I was desperate for Charles to reassure me. He tried to.

"Unless some other evidence comes to light, I think it is very unlikely that you will be found guilty. But, you will be tried in a Crown Court in front of a jury. They will probably realize that there is, at least, a reasonable doubt about your guilt, but you can never be absolutely certain when a jury is involved."

"Fucking hell. How has this happened?" I said, not feeling reassured at all. Charles decided not to even try to answer my question. He told me that it was better if he drove me back home and that we meet up again the next day when we would both be thinking more clearly. Before we left the pub, we arranged to see each other at his house the following afternoon.

On the way back to London, I asked Charles a few questions which, essentially, were just the same questions I had asked earlier but in a rehashed form. For most of the journey, I was contemplating what I would say to Jilly when I got home. I couldn't imagine a more difficult conversation. Not only did I need to tell her that I had been unfaithful, I needed to tell her that I had been unfaithful with one of our closest friends who had then accused me of rape. Even worse than that, I needed to explain that I had been arrested for that rape and that I was only a free man because I had been released on police bail. I knew that I couldn't give Jilly the time to focus on my adultery before I told her about the rape allegation. She would no doubt react very badly to my infidelity, but the plain fact was that my arrest was going to have a much greater impact on her, the boys – all of us.

—

I arrived home just before 9 p.m., which gave me plenty of time to practice how I would break the news to Jilly. She had texted me to say that she wouldn't be home before 10 p.m. I planned to welcome her home with a glass of wine before I dropped my bombshell. I paced up and down the sitting room practicing different versions of what I was going to say. I finally settled on:

*Jilly I have to talk to you about something very important. Well, in fact, it's two things. The first is my responsibility, the second is not. I am in serious trouble. Please can you listen to everything I have to say before you speak. You will feel like interrupting me after I have told you the first thing, but please don't. You need to hear everything.*

Realistically, I knew that Jilly would want to interrupt me before I had even finished my first sentence. I had to ignore her, even shout over her if necessary, and just continue until I had, at least, got these first few sentences out. The first few sentences were, of course, the least of my worries. I then had to tell her about what had happened between Rosie and I, and then what I had been accused of. I decided to be blunt and use as few words as possible on the basis that this would give me the best chance of saying everything I needed to. I practised a bit more while looking at myself in the mirror above the fireplace.

*After you and Mark left the Cottage, something happened which I regret more than I can tell you. Rosie and I spent the day together and then we had sex on Sunday night. This morning the police arrested me on suspicion of having raped Rosie. I can only assume that Rosie told Mark that we'd had sex and he forced her to go to the police claiming that she has been raped in order to get back at me. That is the only explanation I can think of as to why she would have made up such a terrible lie. You know how Mark can be if things go against him. He becomes vicious. You also know that Rosie does whatever Mark tells her to. Please believe me when I say that I profoundly regret having sex with Rosie. I have betrayed you, but I want to make it clear that the sex between Rosie and I was completely consensual. I did not rape her. I repeat…. I did not rape her.*

I was quite pleased with what I had come up with and therefore decided to say more.

*The police have released me on bail, but I have to return to the police station in four weeks time. I called Charles Burton when I was arrested and his best advice was that he thinks I will face trial but that I will be found not guilty. He believes in my innocence, but I need you to believe me too. I did not rape her and I need your support. Please help me.*

Of course, things did not go to plan. Jilly got back home just after 10 p.m. and while I stood in the sitting room she walked straight past the open door without looking into the room. She was talking on her mobile and all I got in response to my greeting was a derisory wave of her hand. She went straight to the kitchen and I heard her open the fridge door, grab herself a bottle and pour a glass of wine. Her conversation went on for, what seemed, an eternity and while I waited for her to finish I rehearsed my planned monologue. Jilly's call lasted so long that by the time she had finished, her glass of wine was obviously empty and I heard her open the fridge to get a refill. Finally, she left the kitchen and made her way along the hall towards me. As she made her approach, I took a deep breath and got ready to tell her my news. As she appeared in the doorway I moved towards her to give her a kiss, but before I could get to her, let alone start speaking, she recoiled away from me.

126

"Oh my God! What's happened to your face?"

I had completely overlooked the fact that the state of my face would obviously be the first thing that Jilly would want to talk about, and her question threw me off course. I was thrown further off course by Jilly bursting into tears. She moved across the room with one hand stretched out towards me as if she wanted to touch my face. I instinctively moved towards her and took her in my arms briefly before taking a step back and attempting to start my planned explanation.

"I'm fine, it looks a lot worse than it is."

"What happened? Who did this to you?"

The fact that I had forgotten about the state of my face meant that Jilly, completely understandably, was demanding that I start my explanation of what had happened over the last forty-eight hours with something that I hadn't even planned to mention. I tried to get things back on track.

"Jilly, I *will* tell you what has happened to my face, but first I need to tell you something very important. I am in serious trouble and I need you to sit down and listen to me." The expression on Jilly's face changed from one of concern to one of accusation .

"What have you done?"

Finally I was able to start telling Jilly what had happened from the beginning. I decided not to mention in any detail the time that Rosie and I had spent together as this seemed to me to be unnecessarily provocative. I simply said that we had got drunk and ended up having sex. Jilly, once more, surprised me with her reaction. She immediately got up from the sofa and slapped me hard across my bruised face and said, in a calm and detached voice, "You always did fancy her didn't you? I've always known that if you ever got the chance with Rosie then you would take it. You're pathetic."

I was shocked by how hard Jilly hit me, but I knew that I had to tell her the rest of my story. As calmly as possible, I began, "Jilly, I understand that you are upset but you need to calm down and let me speak. After I got home on Monday I dropped into The Red Lion for a quick—"

"Fuck off, Tom. I'm not interested in what you have to say. It'll only be lies. You had to do it didn't you?"

"Do what?"

"You had to get even. No, not even. You had to get your *revenge*. I was wrong doing what I did, but it was a moment of weakness. You had to do something worse didn't you? Rosie is my *best* friend. How could you do it?"

Jilly's anger had turned to distress and she looked to be on the verge of tears. I wanted to reach out to her, to comfort her in some way, but I knew that she would not welcome any physical contact with me at this stage. I also knew that I had to use this lull in her tirade against me to tell her about my arrest. I could not get any words out before Jilly continued, "You've been caught haven't you? The only reason you'd be telling me what you and Rosie have been up to is if Mark has found out. There's no way you'd come clean unless you had to. That's why your face is such a mess, isn't it? Mark has somehow found out what you two have been up to and has given you a good beating."

I was amazed that Jilly had worked out that it was Mark who was responsible for my injuries. I pleaded with her to let me speak for a moment. Despite a few more angry comments, she did finally relent and allow me to continue. I confirmed that it *was* Mark who had beaten me up and that I could only presume that Rosie had told him what had happened because she was feeling guilty. I then quickly told her my theory as to what had happened next. I explained that Mark would not have been able to stand the fact that *his* wife had slept with someone else, and that because that *someone* was me it would have driven him completely mad. I added that he could never stand it when I got the upper hand on him.

All the while that I was talking, Jilly was standing in front of me, with her hands on her hips, looking impatiently at me. It was obvious that she didn't understand why I was giving her this information when the only relevant thing was that I had betrayed her. I knew she wouldn't let me talk much longer without her interrupting me, so I cut to the chase.

"Rosie has accused me of raping her."

Jilly's demeanour changed immediately and completely. Her hands dropped from her hips and hung loosely by her side, the colour drained from her face and she started to breathe heavily. When she finally spoke her voice was barely audible.

"What?"

I repeated that Rosie had accused me of raping her. Then explained that I could only imagine that she had told Mark, and that because his pride had been so wounded, he had forced her to make this claim. Jilly stumbled backwards and sat down on the couch. From this point onwards she was completely silent as I told her about the arrest and everything that had happened up until the moment I had left the police station. For the most part, Jilly sat with her head in her hands. She looked up occasionally and I used these brief moments of eye contact to reassure her of my innocence. When I had finished I sat down in the armchair behind me and stared at Jilly. She was silent for a long time until finally she looked up at me and started crying.

When I tried to comfort Jilly, she pushed me away. She cried on and off for an hour or so. Her sobs were punctuated with disbelieving repetitions of the awful accusations. It was as if she couldn't get her head around what had happened or how she should react to it. Over and over again she murmured, "If you hadn't had sex with Rosie, none of this would have happened."

This was obviously something that I couldn't argue with. There was no disputing this fact and, therefore, I just remained silent. Every time Jilly asked "Why would Rosie accuse you of rape?" I repeated my theory that Mark had forced her to do so in order to get some sort of sick revenge on me. When she asked me, which she did several times, "Did you rape her?" I responded in an increasingly irate way. At first I just answered, "No" but when she repeated the question a second, third and fourth time I answered with increasing indignation and, eventually, exasperation and resentment.

"For the fourth time: no, I did not rape Rosie. I know you don't want to hear this right now, but it is important that I make it very clear. After you and Mark left on Sunday morning, Rosie and I spent a very intimate day together, which culminated in us making love. The sex we had was completely consensual. I am guilty of betraying you, but I am not guilty of rape. I don't deserve what is happening to me because I am completely innocent of committing any crime. I need you to help me, Jilly. I am so sorry that I gave into the moment, but we can deal with that later. Right now, I am in serious trouble and I need your help. There is a chance I could go to jail simply because Mark wants revenge for me sleeping with Rosie. Please, help me."

Jilly sat there with her head down, staring at the carpet. Finally, after what seemed to be an interminable silence, she looked up, stared straight into my eyes and asked, "Do you love her?"

It was not what I was expecting at all and for a brief moment I was dumbstruck. Eventually I gathered myself, looked straight back at Jilly and said, "No…….. I love you."

She immediately got to her feet and stood in front of me. I still didn't know what to expect, but I stood up as well. She closed the gap between us with one small step, wrapped her arms around me and held me very tightly. The release of pressure I felt was overwhelming. I hadn't realised how important it was to me to have Jilly's support and love. For the first time since the police had knocked on the door of our house, I felt that maybe, just maybe, things would be all right.

# Chapter 13

*Total support from Jilly*

Jilly and I held each other for a long time before either of us spoke. I felt a huge sense of relief at, not only having told Jilly of the events of the last couple of days, but also having her believe my version of events. It was me who finally broke the silence with the offer of another glass of wine. She nodded and I led her by the hand into the kitchen. I poured us both a large glass of Chablis and we stood on either side of the kitchen block. Neither of us said anything. It was me who broke the silence once more, partly to suggest that we share an omelette but mostly to divert Jilly from asking me any more questions. I was completely exhausted and just couldn't face another cross-examination. I had been answering questions all day from Charles, the police and Jilly. Thankfully, Jilly seemed to be as exhausted as me and asked me to bring the omelette into the sitting room as she was going to watch the television.

When I appeared at the sitting room door with a tray carrying our supper, Jilly looked up at me and smiled, weakly. I sat down next to her and we ate our food without exchanging a word. I stared at the television but I have no memory of what we were watching. I was just hoping that Jilly wasn't going to ask more questions about what had happened between Rosie and me. I knew that Jilly would want to talk about it much more at some point, probably in excruciating detail, but I was desperate not to have the conversation that night. Thankfully, she said nothing until after we had finished eating and when she did speak, it was just to tell me she was going to bed and to ask me whether I was coming too. It was probably only 11 p.m., but I don't think I've ever needed sleep more than I did at that moment and I followed her upstairs.

I undressed quickly and got straight into bed. Jilly went to the bathroom and when she returned I was lying on my back, half asleep. She switched off the lights, got under the duvet and cuddled up next to me. It had been years since we had fallen asleep in each other's arms and I was just about to fall into, what would no doubt have been, an exhaustion induced deep sleep, when I realised that sleep was not what was on Jilly's mind. She lay on her side with one of her legs over mine and her hand on my chest. She played with my chest hair for a while and then began to move her hand down towards my belly. When she started to grind her pubic bone against my thigh and hip I looked down at her in surprise. There was just enough light for me to see her face as she moved her hand from my body to behind my head and pulled me towards her. She kissed me gently on the lips and then opened her mouth and started to kiss me properly. This was not what I was expecting at all, but suddenly sleep was the last thing on my mind.

Jilly began to kiss me more urgently and with a passion that had been missing in recent times from our sex life. I turned slightly towards her and began to run my hand over her back and then down to her buttocks. She began to grind herself against the upper part of my thigh again. I was just about to roll her over onto her back when she pulled away from me. At first I wondered exactly what was happening, but when she moved on top to sit astride me I thought that whatever she was intending, I was very happy to go along with it. She sat on my stomach and looked down at me. Then she leaned forward and started kissing me again. Simultaneously she reached out behind her and down towards my penis. She was in charge and I was enjoying the feeling.

As quickly as she had sat astride me she then slid herself down my body parted my legs and kneeled between them. She then moved her head forward and took me in her mouth. It was as if the clock had been turned back ten years. In the space of a few minutes I had been transformed from a middle-aged man desperate for sleep into feeling like a teenager. I wanted to make sure that Jilly would get as much pleasure as I was and tried to move her from the position between my legs. Jilly briefly stopped what she was doing and told me to stay exactly where I was. As I came in her mouth, I arched my back. I thrust over and over again into her. Once I had recovered my composure, Jilly grinned at me and trotted off to the bathroom. When she returned, I was still lying on my back. She slid under the covers and positioned herself in exactly the same way as she had when she first came to bed. This time we did fall asleep in each other's arms.

When I woke up the following morning, the sun was streaming through the gaps in the curtains. I couldn't immediately feel Jilly next to me. It flashed through my mind that perhaps she had already gone to work, but when I turned around she was lying next to me. I had turned around with such force that Jilly woke up with a start. She seemed a bit dazed at first, but when she started smiling I was reassured. I reached out towards her, stroked her face and moved towards her. She looked beautiful and I was immediately turned on. This time, I would be in control.

As she lay there on her side I began to kiss her face, and then her lips while gently stroking her back. As soon as she responded to my kisses I manoeuvred her so that she was lying on her back. There was far less urgency to our kisses than the previous night, but just as much passion. I ran my right hand over her breasts and stomach while I cradled the back of her head in my left hand. As I moved my hand down her body, Jilly's legs parted. I resisted the temptation to immediately put my hand between her legs and caressed her belly with circular movements and then moved back to her breasts. Jilly could obviously wait no longer and she guided my hand downwards. She gasped as I slid my fingers inside her, while I continued to kiss her. I was desperate to be properly inside her, but was determined to make her come before I did. She moved against the rhythm of my hand until her pelvis started to buck gently. As she did this, I stopped kissing her so I could watch her face. Her orgasm was accompanied by low moans and as she came she dug her heels into the bed and raised her hips. When I finally got on top of her she was smiling again and seemed desperate for me. As I thrust inside her, she raised her knees to her shoulders and groaned. It didn't take long for me to come but, to me, it seemed to be exactly the right amount of time and as I collapsed in a heap back on to the bed I knew that Jilly felt the same. I also felt certain that I would have her total support over the coming weeks.

# Chapter 14

## *Explanations*

Jilly and I went back to sleep after our lovemaking and when we woke up it was after 9 a.m. I couldn't remember the last time that Jilly hadn't been out of the house by 8 a.m., but that morning, work was not her number one priority. We decided that we needed to give some thought to the practicalities of our situation, so we both rang in sick.

We sat at the breakfast table, drinking coffee. Jilly had a paper and pen in front of her. She was intent on making a list of the things we needed to handle, but before she did that she wanted to know exactly what happened at the police station. She was, for obvious reasons, most interested in what I had told the police about having sex with Rosie and whether they had told me precisely what Rosie had accused me of doing.

It was excruciating recounting exactly what questions I had been asked and how I had answered them. Jilly had declared her total faith in me in the most surprising way, but she was not satisfied with me glossing over any of the intimate details. I felt that, however awkward and embarrassing, I owed it to her to be completely frank and honest. When I had finished, Jilly made a point of saying, once again, that if I hadn't had gone to Rosie's room that "none of this would have happened." I thought it was wise for me to say nothing in response to this even though the silence following Jilly's statement seemed to go on forever. Eventually she picked up her pen and started writing.

At the top of her list were the boys and the painful, but very necessary, job of telling them what had happened. We decided that we needed to phone their housemaster, Mr Woodgate, immediately and tell him that we needed to see him urgently and that we needed to have an equally urgent meeting with the boys. Our thought process was that, at some point, it was possible that the boys could find out from their fellow pupils what had happened. We needed to speak to them first. The plan was that they would come home for a week so they could ask all the questions they needed to and so that they would have appropriate ways of dealing with any comments from the other boys. We wanted to see Mr Woodgate first in order to ask his advice. He was an experienced housemaster and we valued his opinion although, in retrospect, it was pretty obvious that he was highly unlikely to have faced a situation even remotely like this.

John Woodgate had, at first, tried to fob me off with an appointment at the end of the week, but when I told him that I needed to relay some news to the boys that could have a devastating effect on them, he relented. It was agreed that we would meet him just before evening prep started so that he would be certain that when our meeting was over, the boys would be in their rooms doing their homework. When, later that day, we made the journey south to the boys' school in rural

Hampshire, I was as nervous as a child on their first day at a new school. Jilly and I had gone over all the various reactions that we might get from Max and Sam, but we realised that the reality would probably be very different from anything we could plan for. We concluded that it was probably best not to second guess their reactions and it was this fear of the unknown that was making me nervous. I was far less nervous about the response from Mr Woodgate. He could judge me in any way he liked, it was my sons' reactions that mattered to me.

As we drove through the school gates and along the oak tree lined drive, we could see that the school was its usual hive of activity. There must have been at least ten games of rugby being played on the pitches either side of the drive. I suddenly realised that, under more normal circumstances, I would know whether the boys were playing a match against another school and which team they were in. As I looked to my right I could see, in the distance, the Victorian cricket pavilion, which had recently been painted in the traditional pink. Some of the leaves on the trees around the pavilion had started to sport autumn colours. It was an idyllic scene, which, somehow, made the awful situation in which I found myself even more grim. Worse still, was the fact that I would soon be shattering this idyll for my sons.

After a couple of hundred yards, we turned a corner and the main school building came into view. It had been built in the mid-Victorian era and was unusual in its design compared to contemporary buildings. While it was predominately constructed of red brick, it was built in a very grand style. I remember being told when we first visited the school that it was designed in a style loosely termed 'French Grand Rococco.' Normally, when I arrived at the main building, I would stop for a while to marvel at the grandness of it all, but not on that day. On that day I was just focused on the damage that would be caused to my sons and for the first time I had feelings of hatred for Rosie and especially for Mark.

Mr Woodgate greeted us with typical, enthusiastic bonhomie. He was about forty, pick-thin, pale and prematurely balding. His thinness was, as far as I could see, due to the fact that he was always on the 'go'. Not only was he a housemaster and a father of three, he also taught Maths, coached rugby and hockey and ran the drama club. In order to fit all this in, he literally had to run from the boarding house, to the sports field, to the classroom and then back to the house. He led us into his study, sat us down and began to tell us about the progress that Max and Sam were making. I let him talk for only a few seconds, before I stopped him.

As it turned out, poor old Woodgate was completed shocked by what I had to say. As I had expected, he had never been faced with a scenario anything like the one he had been presented with.

"Yes, yes, very unfortunate," was all he could stutter, "Very difficult. Um. Um. Not really sure what to do for the best."

In the end, I realised that I was going to have to take charge of the situation and tell him what was going to happen. I told him that I was going to speak to the boys without him present and then that I would take them home where they would stay until the next weekend. I advised him that he should inform the headmaster of the situation, but no one else. Woodgate nodded vigorously as I spoke. When I told him that I would return the boys to school early the following Monday morning, at which time I wanted to have a meeting with him and the headmaster, he told me that he would arrange the meeting. He seemed very relieved that someone was telling him what would happen and what he needed to do.

When Max and Sam arrived in Woodgate's study they looked ashen-faced. They obviously thought that they were either in serious trouble or that something dreadful had happened. As soon as they saw us both there and I had reassured them that the cuts and bruises on my face were nothing to worry about, their relief was visible. They still looked a bit concerned however, as it was unusual for us to visit them without prior warning. They were, of course, right to be concerned, it was just that it was me in trouble and not them. I made sure that they knew this from the outset.

"Sit down, boys, and please don't look so worried. You are not in any trouble and no one is ill," I explained.

They both smiled and sat down on the sofa. I immediately thought that perhaps I shouldn't have been so reassuring, bearing in mind what I was about to tell them, but on the other hand there was no 'correct' way to tell them about what had happened. I asked Mr Woodgate to leave us. Jilly and I sat in the matching armchairs, which faced the sofa across the coffee table.

"What is it? Why are you here?" asked Sam.

I responded quickly and directly, "I have been accused of something that I haven't done and mum and me thought it was best that we tell you face to face what has happened rather than risk you hearing it second-hand from someone else."

The worried looks returned to both of the boys' faces, but they said nothing and I used this silence to offer some reassurance and, more importantly, some detail.

"First of all, I would like to emphasise that I am completely innocent of what I have been accused of."

"What is it that you have been accused of?" said Max, with a mixture of fear and impatience.

"Well, you know that we went away for the weekend with Mark and Rosie to the West Country?"

"Yes," they chimed in unison.

"Well, mum and Mark had to leave unexpectedly on Sunday morning because of work commitments and Rosie and I stayed in Wiltshire. The long and short of it is that, on Sunday, Rosie and I had a bit too much to drink and ended up doing something very silly. We had sex with each other. It was completely consensu—"

Before I could finish what I was saying, Max stood up and started shouting at me, "You arsehole! You total arsehole! I don't see how you can possibly say you've been accused of something you haven't done when you obviously *have* done it. You've *just* admitted it."

I was completely taken aback by Max's reaction. He had never spoken to me in this way before, and it shocked and saddened me. Thankfully, at this point Jilly took over.

"Darling, please. That's not it. Your father isn't denying having had sex with Rosie. He is denying what Rosie has accused him of *after* they had sex."

"What do you mean?" said Max.

Jilly started at a point in the story that I would never have thought of. She told the boys that Mark had attacked me in a pub in London on Monday night. She went on to say that we presumed that Rosie had told him what had happened and that he was jealous and angry. She then explained that when the police had arrived at our house the next morning, I had assumed that someone had reported Mark for beating me up and that they wanted to take a statement from me. In a very straightforward way, Jilly then described that, in fact, the police had come to arrest *me* because Rosie had accused me of raping her. When Max tried to interrupt, Jilly raised her voice and said that we believed that the only possible reason for Rosie to make this accusation was that she had been forced to do so by Mark.

I sat in complete silence while Jilly spoke and I watched the boys to see how they reacted. Max had calmed down and was sitting forward in his chair staring, without expression, at the coffee table. Sam sat back in on the sofa with his arms folded. I could see that he was on the point of tears and the difference in the boys' reactions struck me. Max, at sixteen, was an angry and defiant teenager while Sam, at thirteen, was still a little boy who was just very, very upset. When Jilly went over to Sam, sat next to him on the sofa and put her arm around him, he burst into tears. As I sat in the armchair facing my family, I felt an overwhelming sense of guilt. I knew that for the next few months at least, we were all going to go through very difficult times. Uppermost in my mind was the fact that if I hadn't given in to my urge to have sex with Rosie then none of this would be happening. I could tell from the look on Max's face that he was thinking exactly the same thing.

Both of the boys wanted to ask questions of me as we sat in Woodgate's study. Jilly explained to them that there would be plenty of time for questions over the next few days as we were taking them home with us until the following Monday. Max immediately objected, saying that he had been selected for the first time that season for the under sixteen 'A' team and there was no way he was going to miss the match on Saturday. I had to stop myself from shouting at him. He seemed more interested in playing in a rugby match than the fact that his father could be going to jail. I stopped myself just in time from bellowing at him. I realised that he was right. There was no need for them to stay at home for more than a couple of days. That was plenty of time for me to answer their questions and to prepare them for anything that might be said to them by other boys. It was better from their perspective that they got back to normality as soon as possible.

—

The next couple of days were awkward, to say the least. Max wanted to know as much detail as possible about what had happened. He asked me several times, "How could you have done this to mum?" This was a question to which I had no answer and I could tell that he was disgusted by my behaviour. Thankfully, while he was in no doubt that I had acted immorally, he was also in no doubt that I was innocent of any crime. The questions he asked regarding what was likely to happen next – in terms of whether I would be charged and have to go to court – were easier to answer. They were made easier because, the day after the boys came home, Jilly and I had a meeting with Charles. This helped me gain some clarity as to exactly what I was likely to face.

At that meeting, Jilly and I discussed, in more detail, exactly what we needed to do over the next month and what to expect when I returned to the police station to answer bail. It was Jilly who led the meeting rather than me or Charles. I don't suppose that under normal circumstances Charles would have allowed his client's wife to lead the meeting, however the friendship between the three of us meant that this was not a normal scenario. First of all, she wanted to know precisely what Rosie claimed had actually happened in the bedroom. Listening to Charles explain what Rosie had accused me of was excruciating, but not as excruciating as when she asked me for my version of events. She wasn't satisfied with me saying that the sex was consensual, she wanted to know everything. I suppose I knew that this moment was coming; the moment when I would have to describe in detail how Rosie and I made love, I just didn't think it would happen in Charles' office. Under almost any other circumstances, where infidelity had been uncovered, I could have got away with a perfunctory description of the actual sex act, but this was not one of those circumstances. Jilly sat in complete silence as I described, in exactly the same words as I had used with the police and Charles, my version of events. It was an awful experience for both of us.

Jilly wanted to know exactly where and how I had touched and kissed Rosie. How she had reacted to my caresses, what noises she had made, where she had touched me and, finally, whether she had orgasmed. When I answered, a little disingenuously, that I didn't know, I thought that Jilly might have finished questioning me, but the worst was still to come.

"How much did you enjoy fucking Rosie?" Jilly asked.

I realised that this was a question that I was not going to be asked in court, but also realised that it was one I was going to have to answer. I tried to find words that were believable but not too provocative for Jilly. When I finally came up with, "It was enjoyable," I immediately knew that I had failed on both fronts.

The rest of the meeting with Charles was a little less stressful. He explained that unless somebody had, unbeknown to either Rosie or I, walked passed Rosie's bedroom as we had sex that there could be no other witnesses to the incident. That meant that the only evidence that the police could consider was the evidence already provided by Rosie and myself. The case would, therefore, be passed to the CPS almost immediately.

"If the CPS decide to charge, you will be bailed to appear at a magistrates' court in about ten days time," Charles explained, "Then there will be a hearing, and the case, because of its seriousness, will be sent to the Crown Court. The Crown Court process will probably take three months before a trial actually takes place."

At this point, and probably in anticipation of Jilly asking the obvious question, Charles reiterated what he had already told me, "Despite the fact that the only witnesses to the event were Rosie and yourself, and despite the fact that it would all boil down to her word against yours, you will, in all probability, be charged and therefore the case *will* go to the Crown Court."

The whole process, Charles informed us, should take four to five months. When Jilly asked if that was the longest period of time it would take, Charles replied that it was the length of time it *should* take, not necessarily the length of time it *would* take. He went on to say that it wasn't an exact science and that there was a chance that the whole thing would not be concluded for eight or so months. When he said that this was, of course, assuming that there were no complications, Jilly was very anxious to know what complications there could be. Charles came up with a whole list of things that included extra evidence being presented, delays by the CPS and delays in getting court dates. The elephant in the room was, of course, whether I was likely to be convicted. When Charles was asked this question he wasn't willing to commit one hundred percent to anything. He told us that you can never be absolutely sure when a jury is involved, but as things stood there were no evidential reasons to indicate that a conviction was likely. Rather than reassure me, this actually had the opposite effect, but for Jilly's sake I kept this to myself.

When we got home the boys bombarded me with questions. Thankfully there was no need to go into the type of detail Jilly had demanded earlier in the day. We had made the decision on the way back in the car to be as positive as possible about my prospects. Sam was more than happy to believe us when we said there was very little chance of me being convicted, while Max was a bit more sceptical. The upshot was, however, that they seemed less worried than they had been when we left them earlier in the day. We took them out that evening to a local Italian restaurant and we all got a bit tiddly. Jilly and me on about two thirds of a bottle of red each and Max on about two glasses. I think Sam was more intoxicated by the thought of having an alcoholic drink than the two small sips he actually had. Max walked home with his arm wrapped protectively around Jilly, while Sam held my hand. It was very strange, but this was the happiest time we had spent together as a family for a long time. The next few months were to take an awful toll on all of us, but, for that evening, we were able to shut out our fears and be hopeful.

Jilly and I both rang in sick again on Friday morning and spent the day with the boys. In the morning we played football on Parsons Green and then had lunch in the pub that overlooks it. In the afternoon the boys played computer games and Jilly and I answered a few work emails. In the evening we all went to the cinema. We saw a film called *Avatar* and, to their great amusement, the boys decided that I looked a bit like the humanoid extra-terrestrial beings that were the subject of the film. I feigned outrage at being compared to ten foot tall, blue-skinned humanoids, but actually, I thought that they were pretty impressive beings and secretly I didn't mind the comparison. The more cross I pretended to be, the more the boys laughed.

At various times during the day, the boys asked questions about different aspects of my arrest and what might happen next. Both Jilly and I were as positive as possible in our responses. Jilly, in particular, was able to impress upon them that Rosie's claims were ridiculous and that everything would work out well. It was more difficult to allay their fears about the kids at school finding out what had happened and asking questions or teasing them. Mark and Rosie had friends who had kids at the school and it was only a matter of time before news leaked out. The best advice we could offer the boys was to ignore any teasing or bullying and report any incidents to Mr Woodgate. We also told them that they should contact us immediately if anything was said.

Early on Saturday morning we took the boys back to school in time for their first lessons. Jilly and I had a meeting with Mr Woodgate and the headmaster. They agreed with us that it was best if we kept things as normal as possible for the boys and that it was preferable that they were kept as busy as possible. If any comments were made to either of them about the situation then we would "cross that bridge when we came to it." In the afternoon we flitted between the under fourteens 'B's rugby match, which Sam was playing in, and the under sixteens 'A' match that Max was playing in. Sam scored a try, which delighted him, and although Max's team lost, he seemed happy with his performance. After their matches, I was relieved to see them mucking around with their friends at tea. When we left, they seemed happy and relaxed. I would've known if they were just putting on brave faces.

# Chapter 15

## *More explanations*

One of the things we had spoken to Charles about was the likelihood of my arrest and possible prosecution being in the newspapers. He explained that the press normally looked for something or somebody in which the public would be particularly interested. Neither Rosie, nor I, were in any way high profile. We weren't former pupils of a famous public school or past students at a renowned university. We came to the conclusion that, on that basis, there was unlikely to be press interest. However, Charles said that there was often no particular reason why some cases were widely reported and others not at all. Therefore, we decided that we could not take the chance that either Jilly's parents or my father would read about the case without us having pre-warned them. We recognised that we had to tell them as soon as possible.

My father, Mike, was typically stoic and supportive when I told him the news. He criticised me for having betrayed Jilly, but there was not even the vaguest hint from him that he didn't believe my story. He had known Mark from our schooldays and agreed wholeheartedly that he was capable of bullying Rosie into making her accusations. He wanted me to know that he would help me in any way possible. He had always dealt with a crisis in a matter-of-fact, logical way. The only time I had seen him lose the plot was five years earlier when my mother had died. He had tried so hard to maintain a stiff upper lip, and he had managed it until one Sunday about six months after my mother's funeral.

He had come over for lunch and, as usual, seemed to be in high spirits. He had made sure that since my mother's death that he had kept himself busy with all sorts of activities in his local community. That Sunday, however, he broke down. He and I had gone for a walk after lunch and everything seemed normal. We talked about sport and politics. I lied about how well work was going and he told me all about the latest gossip at his golf club. I mentioned something about mum disliking all the silly politics at the golf club and he just stopped in his tracks. I didn't notice at first and carried on walking for a few moments until I realised he wasn't at my side. I turned around to see him standing stock-still with his head bowed. I rushed back to him and asked if everything was okay. He said nothing at first, and just kept staring at the ground. I reached out to him, put my hand on his shoulder and asked him again if everything was okay. Again, there was silence and I was beginning to worry that he was having a stroke or a heart attack, until he looked up and simply said, "I miss her terribly."

I reached out towards him and put my arms around him. He did the same and we stood there holding each other. Neither of us said anything. It occurred to me that I couldn't remember him having hugged me like that since I was a child. This was not because he didn't love me, but because that sort of physical contact between two grown men was alien to him. He then started to cry, noiselessly at first, and then with low, rhythmical sobs. We stayed in our embrace for a couple of minutes until he went silent, straightened up and gently extricated himself from my arms.

"I am a stupid bugger," he said.

We continued on our walk and talked about my mother until we got back to the house. Neither of us has ever spoken about that moment since.

—

When we broke the news to Jilly's parents, the reaction was markedly different from the one that we'd got from my father. Her father, John, was completely silent, while her mother, Anne, immediately erupted into hysterical sobs. Anne, who was best described as self-absorbed, poisonous and aggressive, seemed more concerned about the shame that would be heaped on her family rather than the fact that Jilly had been betrayed and I had been falsely accused of a terrible crime. She talked about not being able to show her face at their local church or at the tennis club, where both she and John were members. She went on to describe how people, even if they didn't say anything, would be talking about it behind her back and that she didn't think she could bear it. I felt like telling the selfish old witch where to go, but in deference to Jilly's feelings, all I said was a sarcastic, "I understand how dreadful this is for you, Anne, and that's why we have made this special trip to see you."

John shot me a look that let me know that he wasn't best pleased with my tone. Even if he disagreed with his wife, he always supported her in public. Anne, on the other hand, didn't pick up on the sarcasm at all.

"How could you have done such a thing to us," she responded, "I *always* knew you were no good for Jilly and that you couldn't be relied upon and now you've proved me right. I don't think I'll be able to show my face ever again. You've ruined everything, Tom."

I was about to respond to Anne with an even more sarcastic apology, when Jilly spoke for the first time since we had arrived at her parents' house.

"I wouldn't worry about your friends finding out for the time being, mum. Our lawyer says it's unlikely that this will reach the papers even if it does go to trial, although of course if Tom goes to jail then that could change things. Let's hope, *for your sake*, that doesn't happen."

"Well, let's hope not," said Anne, without giving the vaguest indication that she recognised that Jilly might be angry at her reaction.

Shortly after this exchange, we claimed that we had to leave as we had a meeting with our solicitor back in London. Anybody normal would have realised that it was highly unlikely that a meeting with a solicitor would take place on a Sunday evening, but if I'd learned anything over the years, it was that Anne was not normal.

"Yes I think you'd better leave," she said, "I wish you had never told us."

Anne hadn't asked any questions, such as when I would need to go back to the police station; what was the likelihood of me being charged; when the court case might happen; what was the chance of me being found guilty or anything else. To give him his due, John insisted in showing us out and walked us to the car. Once we were outside the front door, and out of Anne's earshot, he gave Jilly a hug and asked some of the questions that we had expected to be asked. None of us mentioned Anne's extraordinary reaction or our sarcastic responses to her. At his request, Jilly promised to keep John informed of any developments.

The last group of people that Jilly and I considered talking to about the situation were our respective employers. We decided that, at this stage, there was no need for Jilly to tell anyone at her company. There was still a possibility that I wouldn't be charged and that, combined with the fact that there was no crossover between Jilly's colleagues and our friends, meant it was very unlikely that news of my predicament would leak out to anyone at IPW. We obviously didn't know Mark's intentions regarding publicising my arrest, but when we spoke to Charles he said that there were two things to bear in mind. Firstly, Mark would probably have been advised by his solicitor not to talk about it and secondly, that Jilly hadn't been accused of anything. I suppose nowadays we might have thought differently due to the rise of Facebook and Twitter, but as recently as 2009 it was very rare for anybody over forty to use this type of social media.

My situation was, obviously, very different. I had been arrested and accused of a very serious crime. I could have trawled through my employment contract to see if there was anything in there that obliged me to disclose what had happened, but we decided that the best option was disclosure, whether I had to or not. On Monday morning I went into work and at 9 a.m. on the dot I made a call to the HR department and insisted on an immediate appointment with Nicola Ferguson, the head of the department. Nicola was an extremely attractive woman in her early fifties. She had very short hair, which she had allowed to go grey, clear skin and huge brown eyes. She was always immaculately dressed in business outfits that showed off her petite figure without ever revealing too much flesh. I had met her on numerous occasions over the years and she was unfailingly poised, professional and cheerful. She never flirted, well not with me anyway, but she had a way of making you feel interesting and important.

On that Monday morning, however, her poise deserted her. She was her normal cheerful self when I entered her office and greeted me with the usual niceties. I wasn't really listening and, before she could say much more than a few words, I interrupted and told her that I had something very important to discuss with her. The smile disappeared from her face and she stared intently at me with, what I assumed was, her 'concerned' face. I decided that there was no point beating about the bush and presented Nicola with the basic facts. I told her that I had been arrested and accused of rape. I didn't mention any of the circumstances surrounding the accusation made against me, or the reason why my face was a bit of a mess or that I was innocent. Beyond the bare minimum of the facts, all I told her was that I had been released on police bail and was due to return to the police station in a month's time.

Nicola physically recoiled when I told her what I had been arrested for. She sat back in her chair, her face went white and she said nothing for an uncomfortable amount of time. I felt like filling in the silence, but I couldn't think of anything worthwhile to say. Nicola finally broke the silence with a high-pitched, "Um" which she followed with a few more "Um"s in progressively deeper tones. Finally, with the colour having returned to her face, she spoke. She told me that I would be suspended immediately pending an internal investigation and then the criminal investigation. She seemed to have gathered herself, but although the colour had returned to her face, bright red patches began to appear on her neck and the top of her chest. Her voice, however, had returned to normal and she went on to explain that because I had not been remanded in custody and therefore was able to work, I would be suspended on full pay. She finished up by saying that she would confirm the terms of my suspension in writing and that these terms would be reviewed at regular intervals. The meeting was over within a few minutes.

I thanked Nicola, got up from my chair and left her office. I could have asked her all sorts of questions: Who else she would tell in the organisation? Should I speak to my boss before I left? For how long would I receive full pay? But, I had an overwhelming urge to, not only get out of her office, but out of the building. Because I worked for a large corporation, I knew they would do everything by the book, and in the interests of the company. Nicola would, no doubt, get the appropriate legal advice and nobody beyond those who *had* to know, would be informed. I was confident that I would be paid for however long I was off work and that would not stop unless I was found guilty. I walked out of the office knowing that at least over the coming months I wouldn't have any money worries to add to my other worries.

# Chapter 16

## *Limbo*

I felt relief at having spoken to everybody I needed to. It had been a pretty busy time and, one week after the police knocked on my door to arrest me, I at least didn't have to explain myself to anybody else. My relief was, however, replaced by constant worry. I also had absolutely nothing to do. While Jilly was at work and the boys were kept busy at school, I just sat about the house doing nothing. I would wake up each morning with a sick feeling in the pit of my stomach. I didn't even get a few seconds before I started feeling this way, it started as soon as I opened my eyes. I read the newspaper and then watched breakfast television but, if someone had asked me what I had read about or watched for the first hour of my day, I couldn't have told them. My mind was constantly mulling over what had happened and what might happen in the future.

Charles had told me that there was little, if anything, to do before my return to the police station. A couple of times I rang him up to ask whether we should encourage the police to talk to the staff at the Cottage so that they could verify that Rosie and I had been intimate on that fateful Sunday. He told me that we needed to wait until we found out whether the CPS had decided whether or not I was to be prosecuted. He was very patient whenever I spoke to him. He reiterated that there was essentially nothing to be done at this stage and also that, unless there were some significant developments, there was a good chance that I would be prosecuted. He advised me to try and get on with my life, as normally as possible, until this was confirmed. He also advised me to keep a diary.

I didn't initially see the point in keeping a diary, but Charles was adamant that this would be a valuable exercise. He wanted me to record, while it was still fresh in my mind, exactly what had happened to date. It was to document how I felt from the time I first arrived at the Cottage, exactly what had happened between Rosie and I and everything I had told the police. Charles emphasised the importance of consistency. He wanted me to make sure that if, and when, I was interviewed again by the police, every detail should match what I had already said. He made great play of the fact that if I did end up going to court that the prosecuting barrister would exploit any inconsistency.

The diary writing exercise, which Charles insisted I should continue throughout my ordeal, proved to be more valuable than I could have imagined. Firstly, it gave me something to do and a focus. Secondly, it gave the basis for me to recount this story. Charles told me, "Write the diary so that if anybody else were to read it they would have no doubt as to your innocence."

When I wasn't worrying about what was going to happen, I was angry and frustrated. Angry that Rosie had told Mark what had happened rather than speaking to me first. Angry that she hadn't seen what had happened as an opportunity for us to be together. Angry that she had either told Mark that what had happened had been rape, in order that she could assuage her guilt, or alternatively that she had allowed Mark to bully her into claiming that it was. My frustration was that I could do nothing – but wait. After a couple of days of these emotions I felt that my head might explode. On a few occasions I took to repeatedly thudding the heel of my hand into my forehead as if this would, somehow, relieve the pressure. I quickly realised that it was incredibly unhealthy for me to just stay in the house all day long, although I did get some relief from my boredom when Jilly came home from work. We could discuss how her day had gone and make small talk about whatever was on television, but during daylight hours I was alone, and I felt like I was going mad. The solution was to get busy.

I saw a lot of my father in the weeks running up to my return visit to the police station. He was unfailingly supportive, even though we rarely talked about what I was facing. I also took to going to the gym on a daily basis, which was something I hadn't done for ten years. I found that, if I pushed myself hard enough, the pain and exhaustion stopped me from thinking about anything else. On the days that I didn't go to the gym, I played golf with a variety of different people, claiming that I had a day off work. In the evenings I drank too much. I would work my way through one and sometimes two bottles of red wine until I felt that I was numb enough to fall asleep. If there had been anything constructive I could have done to put myself in a better position, I would have done it, but there was nothing I could do at this stage.

One week before I was due to return to the police station, I met up with Charles. I had been desperate for the time to pass so that, at least, I would have the certainty of knowing whether or not I would be charged, but now that it was getting close, gut-wrenching fear was becoming an even bigger part of my life. I met Charles at his house in Primrose Hill while his wife and his kids were out. We sat at his kitchen table and went over all the various possibilities. It was a very homely way to discuss something that could change my life, and the lives of my family, forever.

"How have you been?" asked Charles.

"Not too bad," I lied.

"Good. Now tell me, has anything changed at your end?"

"No, I've just been trying to keep busy and trying not to think about my situation twenty-four hours a day. At least decision day is only a week away."

"Or not."

"What do you mean 'Or not'?"

"Well, there's always a chance that you will be bailed again if they haven't made their decision."

This was a complete body blow to me. I had assumed that, at the very least, I would know one way or another, when I returned to the police station, whether I would be charged. Charles explained that there were a number of reasons why a decision might not have been made. He told me that it was possible that the police had decided to interview the Cottage staff and hadn't been able to complete those interviews, or that the CPS had received the police file but, due to workload, they hadn't had time to look at it.

"So I might be bailed for another month?" I asked.

"Yes, quite possibly. I'm sorry, Tom. I thought you knew that."

"No, I didn't, Charles."

I felt like saying that *of course I didn't fucking know that, I work in IT not in the law*, but I decided that wouldn't be helpful and instead decided that I needed to have a clearer understanding of how things were likely to pan out over the next few days and weeks. As it turned out Charles described a scenario that was likely to unfold over a period of many many months rather than a few weeks.

He explained that I could be bailed again to return to the police station in four, or even six weeks time. That would take me to mid-December or even early January. Then, if I were charged, I would be bailed to attend a magistrates' court for a preliminary hearing. This would take place about three weeks later. At the preliminary hearing the judge would set a timetable for the trial. Charles was in full flow as he described the process and I was grateful for this as it probably prevented him from noticing how I was reacting. All the talk of courts and hearings made me feel physically sick and I'm sure that all the colour had entirely left my face. Thankfully, Charles just ploughed on with his description of the horrors that awaited me.

"The prosecution will be given thirty days to serve their case on the defence. Once this information had been given to the defence lawyer, i.e. me, and the court, the defence lawyer will, in turn, be given twenty-one days to submit the defence statement to the prosecution and the court."

I calculated that by this time it would be late March or early April.

"A week later the plea and case management hearing will take place in the Crown Court," Charles continued, "The trial date will be set at the PCMH and will probably be about two months later."

By my calculations this meant that from arrest to trial could take eight months, and that was assuming there were no unforeseen delays. It occurred to me that in the past, when I'd heard of arrests being made in the press or on television, I had never once thought about the tortuous process involved. It was also the case that I had assumed that the 'accused' was guilty, on the basis that the police wouldn't have arrested them if they didn't have a very good reason. I certainly had never considered that, innocent or guilty, there was the prospect of months or even years of uncertainty, frustration and fear for those accused. When, months or even years after the arrest, the case came to court, I never thought about how long it had taken to get to that stage and how damaging the wait could be to all involved.

# Chapter 17

## *Answering bail*

Finally, the morning of 19th November arrived. I had slept surprisingly well and, by the time I woke up, Jilly was already up and about. She had taken the day off work and had decided to cook me a full English breakfast. When I arrived in the kitchen, she had almost finished cooking the meal. She turned around and smiled weakly at me as I took a seat at the kitchen table. The smell of the cooking would normally have made me salivate, but on that day it just made me feel queasy. I returned Jilly's smile as enthusiastically as I could and thought about how the hell I was going to force down the amount of food being prepared. Jilly brought two huge plates of food to the table and set them down, before sitting down opposite me. I took my first mouthful of sausage and beans and proclaimed that it was delicious. Simultaneously, Jilly had taken her first mouthful, but just after I had complimented her on the fantastic looking breakfast, she put her knife and fork down and told me that she was feeling too nervous to eat any more. I was relieved, as it meant that I could stop my pretence and admit that I couldn't face eating anything either. I picked the plates up, emptied the food into the bin and returned to the kitchen table where all that remained were two steaming cups of tea.

We drank our tea in silence for a while, before tears started to well up in Jilly's eyes. I moved to her side of the table and put my arm around her. She nestled her head into my neck and started to cry. I kissed the top of her head and tried to reassure her.

"It's going to be alright, Jilly."

"But what if it's not? What's going to happen to us, Tom?"

"We're going to be fine. Remember, I haven't done anything wrong and it's only Rosie who says I have. If this does go to court, Charles is very confident that I will be found not guilty."

Charles had not actually said this, but I took the view that there was no need, at this stage, to be anything other than positive about the outcome whenever I discussed it with Jilly. I decided that if it got to court there would be plenty of time to inject more realism and, as far as I was concerned, there was still a reasonable chance that things wouldn't get that far.

"Oh God, I can't bear the thought of this going to court. I don't think I could stand it," Jilly responded.

I was just about to go into full reassurance mode, when the doorbell rang. It was Charles. It had been arranged that he would pick me up and that we would go to Overbury Police Station together. As soon as he entered the kitchen, he could see that Jilly had been crying. He walked straight over to her and gave her a big hug and told her that he would do everything in his power to make sure that justice prevailed. He didn't say I wouldn't be charged, or that the case wouldn't go to court or that I would definitely be cleared if it did, but he did a better job of calming Jilly down than I had.

Maybe it was years of experience or maybe she just trusted him more, but when Charles and I left the house, Jilly was in a much better state of mind.

On the way to Wiltshire, I went over all the possibilities with Charles. He was a man of great patience; because this was the umpteenth time I'd done this over the last month.

"So, it could be that Rosie has withdrawn her evidence and that, therefore, I will not be charged?"

"Possible, but I think that we would have been informed if that were the case."

"But still possible?"

"Yes, possible but unlikely."

"Okay. Alternatively it could be that the CPS have decided that there is not a strong enough case for there to be a reasonable chance of prosecution?"

"Again, possible but unlikely. These days, in a rape case where it is one person's word against another's, the CPS will most often decide to go ahead and prosecute."

"Alright, so the most likely scenario is that they charge me and then I am bailed to appear at a magistrates' court at a future date."

"Correct. Although, there is still an outside possibility that they will charge you and remand you in custody until your court date."

"That's very unlikely though, isn't it?"

"It *is* very unlikely, but it's my duty to let you know that it *is* a possibility."

I was hoping with every fibre of my being that it would be one of the first two possibilities I had suggested, but logic told me that I would be charged. Whilst I was fairly confident that I would be bailed even if I was charged, I was terrified that, for some reason, they'd lock me up until the trial. I was lost in the turmoil of my thoughts right up until the moment that we arrived at the police station and then, all of a sudden, I was calm. A certainty came over me, and I knew that I would be charged and bailed and then I would go home. I was equally certain that, with Charles' help, I would be found not guilty. I walked confidently into the police station.

Charles did the talking when we got to the front desk. He handed over the piece of paper I had been given when I was originally bailed and then I was booked in by the desk sergeant. After having gone through this formality, he asked us to take a seat and then picked up the phone. I looked at Charles to see if there was anything unusual in what was going on and was relieved to see him looking intently at his mobile. The calmness and certainty that I had felt as we had arrived at the police station was beginning to desert me. I heard the desk sergeant speaking to, someone whom I assumed was, Detective Sergeant Lane, informing him that I had arrived. I knew that I was only a few seconds, or at most a few minutes, from knowing what my immediate fate would be. I took a couple of deep breaths and tried to look as composed as possible, although whom I was trying to impress I don't know. I didn't have to wait long, because within a minute, Lane appeared with a uniformed police officer in tow.

Charles and I got to our feet as the two police officers approached and I greeted them with a "Good Afternoon." Lane didn't acknowledge me at all. He looked straight past me and told Charles that he would like to talk to him alone in an interview room. He then turned to his uniformed colleague and told him to take me down to the cells. Once again I looked at Charles for reassurance. He smiled at me and told me to go with the uniformed officer. I wasn't reassured. As we parted company, I asked Charles if this was normal. He shrugged and said something to the effect that it wasn't *abnormal*. Again, I wasn't reassured. As I was led downstairs, I felt panic rising within me. It wasn't particularly that I didn't want to spend any more time in a cell, although that did freak me out a bit, it was that I couldn't imagine why Lane would want to talk to Charles alone. I asked the uniformed guy what was happening, but all he said was that he'd been told to put me in a cell and therefore that was what he was doing.

Once I was in the cell, I managed to calm down again and I told myself that there was no point getting worked up. I convinced myself that there were any number of reasons why Lane wanted to talk to Charles alone, and I ignored the fact that I couldn't think of even one. I sat down, stared at the grey wall in front of me and tried to think about nothing at all, but, as time moved on, I couldn't help thinking that something was amiss. I tried to keep a track of how long I had been in the cell and by the time I'd got up to half an hour I was pacing up and down. I was just beginning to think that maybe they'd forgotten me, when I heard footsteps in the corridor. My cell door opened and there was an ashen-faced Charles. I spoke first.

"It's bad news isn't it? They're going to charge me aren't they?"

"Yes they are, Tom. But you need to prepare yourself for a shock."

"What do you mean, prepare myself for a shock? It's already as bad as it could possibly be."

"No, it isn't, I'm afraid. Please, stay as calm as you can and listen to me very carefully. There has been a second allegation of rape and they are going to re-arrest you for that and then interview you regarding this new allegation. After they have done that, then they're almost certainly going to charge you with both rapes."

I couldn't actually compute what Charles was saying and, initially, I thought that they were going to arrest me for raping Rosie twice. I started to ask how they could possibly be arresting, and potentially charging me, with two counts of rape against the same woman, on the same night, when Charles interrupted me.

"No Tom, you don't understand. There has been a completely separate allegation of rape made by a different woman… do you know of somebody called Tessa Green?"

"What?"

"Do you know a woman called Tessa Green?"

I thought for a moment and then said quietly, "I *did* know her. Many years ago."

"I'm afraid Tom that she has come forward and alleged that you raped her in 1980 when you were at school."

I was dumbstruck by what Charles was saying. I had, at his suggestion, been hoping for the best but preparing for the worst. This, however, was so much worse than the 'worst' scenario that I was unable to think, never mind say anything. Charles tried to calm me down but I was all over the place. I was pacing up and down the cell and when I tried to speak all I could do was make random grunts and gestures. Eventually Charles persuaded me to sit down and started explaining what had been alleged.

"Look Tom, at this stage the police have not told me very much. They are only obliged to disclose the basic details of what has been alleged. What they are saying is that this woman, Tessa Green, came to Overbury Police Station just over a week ago and claimed that you raped her after a school event in 1980. They want to interview you about it now. We need to talk about what you can remember, if anything, about that incident."

I had been sitting with my head in my hands while Charles spoke and the horrible truth of what was happening was slowly dawning on me. All I could respond with was, "I don't fucking believe this. What the fuck is happening?" After a period of silence I finally said, "It's that bastard Mark. He's trying to completely stitch me up."

Charles sternly told me that we needed to concentrate on what I was going to say in the interview and that we could discuss Mark later. He then asked me again what I could remember about the incident with Tessa. Despite my shock, and the fact that it was thirty years ago, it wasn't difficult for me to remember precisely what had happened. You don't ever forget losing your virginity.

"I remember exactly what happened, Charles. I was in the lower sixth and it was the Wednesday before the half term holiday in February 1980. I was nearly seventeen. Every Wednesday night we had something called 'Pops', which meant that we were allowed to go to the school bar, situated in an outbuilding in the grounds of the school, and have a few drinks. We were officially limited to two alcoholic drinks each, but there were no strict controls and most of us, both the boys and the girls, would usually have more than that. I can't remember why Tessa Green was there because she worked at the school rather than being a pupil, but I presume she was helping out behind the bar."

"Were you drunk, Tom?"

"No, at most I was a bit tipsy, but definitely not drunk."

"Ok, carry on."

"There was some music playing and a few of us were dancing. I was dancing with Tessa and it was getting a bit physical."

"What do you mean by that? Were you kissing?"

"No, we weren't kissing. There were a couple of priests there, keeping an eye on us, so we weren't kissing. We were just grinding a bit. Anyway, I was hoping to take it to the next stage, so I suggested we go outside to get some fresh air. Once we were outside and out of sight of the priests we started kissing and fondling each other."

"Did you have sex with her at this point?"

"No. I asked her to stay outside while I went back inside and borrowed the car keys of one of my 'day boy' friends who had driven down to 'Pops'. His car was in the car park. I got the keys, went back outside, and suggested to Tessa that we would be more comfortable in the car. She went willingly with me to the car where we continued kissing and fondling each other. One thing led to another and we ended up having sex."

"Describe to me exactly what happened."

"Well, I was sitting in the driving seat and she was in the passenger seat. We had put the back of the seats down and, after kissing for a while, I unbuttoned her shirt and started to fondle her breasts. Shortly afterwards I unbuttoned my trousers and guided her hand towards my crotch. She started to masturbate me. This continued for a while and then I climbed over the gear stick, got on top of her and we had sex."

"Did you speak to each other while you were in the car?"

"Other than me telling her to get in the passenger side of the car, I don't think we spoke until after we had finished having sex."

"What did you say then?"

"I can't remember exactly, but it was something along the lines of "It's best we don't go back into 'Pops' together. I'll go in first, you come after in a couple of minutes.""

"Did you speak to her once she came back into 'Pops'?"

"She didn't come back in. In fact, I never saw her again. We broke up for half term the next day and then when I got back to school she had left her job."

"Did you try to contact her?"

"No. I know it sounds bad, but I wasn't really that keen on seeing her again. I was desperate to lose my virginity and once we'd had sex I wasn't particularly interested in having any sort of relationship with her."

"How did you find out that she had left her job?"

"Mark told me. Apparently, she had spoken to him before she left."

"Why would she have done that?"

"Mark had a bit of a fling with her the previous year. I suppose you could say that they were going out with each other for a short period, although it would be more accurate to say that he slept with her from time to time for a couple of months. They had remained friends after he stopped sleeping with her."

"What did Mark say to you when he told you that Tessa had left the school?"

"I can't remember."

"Did he indicate in any way, that she was unhappy with what had gone on between the two of you?"

"No."   ·

Charles had been scribbling away on a pad of paper all the time that we had been talking and he asked me to give him a few moments while he read through his notes. Finally he looked up and asked me a final question.

"At any stage did Tessa object to, or resist, what you were doing?"

"No, it was all very much a natural progression from kissing, to fondling, to having sex. I didn't ask her whether I could go on to the next stage, it just happened."

Once Charles had finished asking me questions, it was my turn to ask him some. First of all, I wanted to know what would happen next. He told me that I would now be interviewed by the police about the accusation. He advised me that, much as had been the case when I was interviewed about Rosie's claims, I should just tell the police exactly what I had just told him. He made a point of saying this would constitute 'implied consent'. I felt a bit reassured that he saw the situation as another case of her word against mine. I foolishly presumed that if either of the accusations got to court then I had a good chance of acquittal. When I expressed this view to Charles, he bluntly pointed out that this second accusation completely changed things. He explained that it was likely that I would be tried on both charges together and that the fact that there were two separate charges, made it much more likely that I would be found guilty.

Charles' bluntness left me reeling, but it was his change in attitude towards me that had the most impact. He seemed, to me, to have become cold and detached – even suspicious. If I hadn't known him so well, perhaps I wouldn't have noticed, but I instinctively knew that before I tried to convince the police, a court or a jury of my innocence, I needed to have him totally on my side. I decided that, before I was interviewed by the police, I needed to convince him that Mark must be involved in Tessa coming forward after all these years. I desperately wanted Charles to believe that, not only was I completely innocent, but that I was being set up.

"You *do* realise that Mark is almost certainly behind all this?"

Charles didn't respond, or perhaps I didn't give him the chance to respond.

"He *has* to be involved," I continued, "I can't think of any other explanation. What is the likelihood that Tessa Green would come up with this accusation now? Mark must have tracked her down and persuaded her to come up with these lies. I'm sure he hasn't been in touch with her since she left the school, so he must have, somehow, traced her whereabouts. The only thing I can think of is that he must be paying her. I can't think of any other reason for this to be happening."

Charles seemed to be almost relieved that my attitude had become more confrontational. He asked me for some time to think. We sat, in silence, for what seemed like minutes, but was probably much less, before he finally spoke. He was reassuringly decisive when he told me that I should say in my interview with the police that I believed that Mark was in some way involved in Tessa coming forward. He advised me not to make any specific allegations against Mark at this stage, but that I should get my general suspicions on the record. He was adamant, however, that I shouldn't talk about Mark paying Tessa without any evidence at all. As soon as he had stopped talking, there was a knock on the cell door and a young, uniformed policeman, that I had not seen before, put his head around the door. He asked us if we were ready for the interview and, after a brief glance and nod between Charles and I, we made our way back upstairs to the interview room. This time both Lane and McLean were waiting for us when we arrived. I noticed that Lane had a smug look on his face. He obviously thought that the case against me had become much stronger. He was right.

# Chapter 18

*Re-interview*

The interview started in very much the same way as the one regarding Rosie's allegation. Sergeant Lane briefly outlined the accusation made by Tessa and then asked me to explain, in my own words, what had happened. All the way through my explanation, Lane sat with his arms folded with an almost disinterested look on his face. It was as if he was thinking that my version of events was predictable in its denial of any wrongdoing, but that with two similar allegations he was very much in the driving seat. When I had finished he went on the attack.

"Ms Green's version of events is that when you tried to get on top of her she pushed you away and told you to get off."

"That's not true."

"She said that as soon as she pushed you away, you turned nasty. You called her a – and I'm quoting her words – "cock-teasing bitch" and forced yourself on top of her. Isn't that what really happened, Mr Bishop?"

"Absolutely not."

"Isn't it a bit of a coincidence that you claim that immediately before you had sex with Ms Green no words were exchanged?"

"What do you mean?"

"I mean, that you claimed that no words were

exchanged between you and Rosie Griffiths, before you had sex with her, either."

"I don't know what to say to that, other than there wasn't any conversation on either occasions. It was just a natural progression."

"Ms Green says that she pleaded with you to get off her. Isn't that what really happened, Mr Bishop?"

"No, it isn't."

"And then, when she kept pleading with you to get off her, you put your hand over her mouth and forced her head back."

"That's not what happened."

"Isn't it a bit of a coincidence that both Mrs Griffiths and Ms Green claimed you put your hand over their mouths to prevent them pleading with you to stop."

"That is not what happened."

"Both women claim that you forced their legs up to their chest with your right hand while you covered their mouths with your left hand and raped them. Just a coincidence that their claims are so similar, Mr Bishop?"

I saw my chance to get it on the record that I thought that Mark was in some way behind the accusations made by Rosie and Tessa.

"No. I don't think that it *is* a coincidence. I believe that Mark Griffiths is behind both of these women's claims. I don't understand why he is doing this, but it just seems extraordinary that Tessa Green would come forward with these claims after thirty years. I think Mark Griffiths is infuriated by the fact that I made love to his wife and that he has forced her to claim that I raped her and then, somehow, persuaded Tessa to accuse me as well."

Charles reached out and touched me on the knee. It was an indication that he didn't want me to say any more and the rest of the interview passed off without any surprises. When Lane decided to call an end to proceedings, Charles requested that he have a private consultation with his client. We were left alone and I immediately asked him how he thought things had gone and what was likely to happen next. He told me that he thought that the interview had gone as well as could be expected and that I would probably be bailed to return to the police station in another month or so. This would give the police and CPS more time to gather evidence and make a decision as to whether they would charge me or not. Charles emphasised that with two separate accusations it was highly likely that in due course I would be charged, unless one or both parties withdrew their evidence.

When Detective Sergeant Lane returned, he politely requested that I follow him to the front desk. I had resigned myself to the prospect of at least another month hanging around on bail waiting for a decision. In the event, things happened much more quickly than I had anticipated. I was charged with two counts of rape there and then. I was in a complete daze by the time the desk sergeant finished reading out the charges. I thought that I had prepared myself for this moment, but the cold reality of it hit me like a sledgehammer. I felt sick and weak and, completely unexpectedly, I felt like running away. I had always thought that when people used panic as an excuse for running away from the scene of the crime that it was a pretty weak defence. In fact, I had very much regarded running away as tantamount to admitting guilt, but here I was with an almost overwhelming urge to bolt. Thankfully I didn't have to resist the urge for long because as soon as the desk sergeant finished reading out the charges he informed me that I would be bailed to appear at Westbury Magistrates' Court in ten days time.

# Chapter 19

## *Pre-trial*

In the months leading up to my trial, I found out who my good friends were. I had kept in touch with half a dozen friends from school and it turned out that all but one of them sided with Mark. People, who I thought were good friends, turned out to be enemies. Most of Jilly and I's mutual friends from university distanced themselves. We saw one or two of them in the first couple of months after I was charged and then they became regularly unavailable. I had introduced some of these university friends to Mark over the years and they had become friends with him. These people were progressively hostile to me when I contacted them. None of the people I had worked with over the years were supportive and neither were the 'friends' we had made who were fellow parents at our sons' various schools. As the trial date approached, I realised that I only had three good friends. These were, my one remaining school friend, Joe Donnelly; my dad, who I suppose had no real choice; and Charles, who I was paying.

When I told Jilly that, not only had I been charged with raping Rosie, but also that I had been charged with another rape as well, she reacted very badly. I had been brutally honest with her about the likelihood of Rosie's accusations ending up with me on trial, but the second accusation not only massively increased the probability of me being found guilty it also shook her belief in me. Initially she could not get her head around the idea that Mark was manipulating the whole situation. I could tell that she was beginning to doubt me and that she just couldn't see how Mark could get two women to make false accusations of rape. We had a huge, screaming row about her lack of faith in me, which I found deeply unsettling. I began to realise that, if my own wife was having doubts about believing me, then I had very little chance of convincing a jury that I was innocent. I spent a couple of days feeling very sorry for myself and desperately trying to work out what, if anything, would make the situation seem anything less than completely hopeless. Hope was delivered from a very unexpected place about a week later when Joe Donnelly, the one school friend who hadn't sided with Mark, called me.

Joe was an under-achieving, mean-spirited alcoholic who was ever present at the 'get togethers' that half a dozen of us from St Michael's had every few months. We suspected that he always turned up because he never had anything else to do or anybody else to see. When Joe called me and suggested that we meet up for a drink, I hadn't been out of the house for nearly a week and I leapt at his offer even though he was likely to be less than sparkling company. We met at a pub near Waterloo Station because from there it was easy for him to get the tube down the Northern Line to his flat in Morden. It wasn't particularly convenient for me, but I had plenty of time on my hands and definitely had nothing better to do. When I arrived, it was immediately obvious that Joe had been there for some time because he had that half-lidded look to his eyes, which suggested he'd had a few already.

Joe was of average height with a stocky build, and, as usual, he was bursting out of his dark, pinstriped suit. Whenever I saw him, he seemed to be wearing the same slightly shiny, ill-fitting, cheap suit. I presumed that he didn't actually wear the same one every day, but that he had bought two or three identical ones some years ago when he was considerably slimmer. As I approached him, he gave me his familiar lopsided grin which, to those that didn't know him, looked more like a sneer. His medium brown, medium length, slightly greasy hair was brushed forward and appeared to be stuck to his forehead. When I was within earshot he greeted me with, "Alright wanker, you look like shit."

This was his customary greeting and it made me laugh for the first time in a while. Joe was nothing, if not consistent. He was consistently rude, consistently dismissive of everybody and everything, and consistently miserable. He had worked in the same role as an account manager at a telecommunications company for as long as I could remember and it always amazed me that he had managed to keep his job. He hated the company he worked for, disliked everybody he worked with and was utterly dismissive of the clients that he managed.

On that evening however, it was not only Joe's relentless pessimism, which cheered me up. He said something, which gave me renewed confidence that my theory that Mark was, somehow, behind all my troubles might just have some substance. Joe told me he had been for a drink with Rosie's brother, Patrick, and a couple of other school friends earlier in the week. He went on to say that, perhaps inevitably, the sole topic of conversation was me and what I had allegedly done to Rosie and Tessa. Joe described how Patrick was very, very angry and determined that I should pay the heaviest price for, what he believed, I had done to his sister. He had no doubts about my guilt, but he recognised that a situation where it was one person's word against another, or in this case two others, that there was a possibility that I might "get away with it." According to Joe, Patrick then said something very interesting about Tessa.

Patrick had, somewhat cryptically – although Joe had used the words "talking in fucking riddles," – alluded to Mark having influenced the situation. Apparently, when Phil Henshaw, another St Michael's old boy, had said how appalled he was by what had happened in Wiltshire, Patrick had replied, "Well, as we know, it's not the first time that Bishop has behaved like this. He's got a track record."

When asked by Phil, who was unaware of the second charge of rape, what he meant, Patrick said that just before Tessa had disappeared from school, she had confided in Mark, that "Bishop" was the reason she was leaving. Apparently, Tessa had refused to elaborate at the time, but she had referred to me as a "complete bastard."

"And that was enough for Mark and Patrick to come to the conclusion that I must be guilty of raping Tessa?" I enquired of Joe.

"Patrick didn't *exactly* say that, but he hinted that it was enough for Mark, after what Rosie had claimed you'd done to her, to find out directly from Tessa exactly what had happened all those years ago."

"This is ridiculous. I freely admit that I didn't treat Tessa well. I did fuck her and then fuck off, but I didn't rape her. They have put two and two together and come up with five."

"It sounds like it, but that's not the interesting part of it."

"What do you mean?"

"Patrick then went on to hint that Mark had been to see Tessa and sorted things out with her."

"What exactly did he say?"

"He said something along the lines of "Mark has a way of sorting these things." As I say, Patrick was talking in fucking riddles, but I got the impression that Mark had been in touch with Tessa and persuaded her to come forward... I reckon he's paying her to talk."

At this point, I slammed the palm of my hand on the table and half-shouted, "I fucking knew it! I knew Mark was behind all of this!"

I wanted to ask Joe if he had any evidence that Mark was paying Tessa, but decided not to ask more questions or tell him what I intended to do with this information just in case it somehow got back to Mark. I trusted Joe, but felt it was safer not to share too many of my thoughts with him. It also occurred to me that Joe's hatred of Mark could be colouring his views. Mark had always treated him with utter contempt. While 'banter' was an important part of the fun of meeting up with old school friends, Mark took things too far with Joe.

'Bullying' has become an increasingly overused term, but there was no other way of describing how Mark treated Joe. At every opportunity he would confront him with his lack of success in his career, his life and with women. Joe had never introduced us to any of the women he claimed to be dating and Mark would regularly humiliate him about this. In fact for a period of about two years Mark openly called him "queer Joe" and would ask him the name of his latest "imaginary girlfriend." Mark would then go on to explain, in a loud voice, why Joe had to "make up" girlfriends and why, whenever we were in mixed company, he was so obnoxious to women. According to Mark, it was because he was a misogynist and his misogyny was driven by his homosexuality. Mark would always conclude by saying that, "The reason why you're called 'queer Joe' is, of course, because you're a fat, ugly queer." The unfortunate Joe had no real comeback and it was painful to witness. Perhaps I should have defended him, but I always thought that this would probably have made things worse.

For the rest of the evening I spent with Joe, I guided the conversation away from anything related to my upcoming date at the magistrates' court and Joe's theories about Mark. We talked about all sorts of things, but I thought about only one thing. I needed to talk to

Charles about what I had heard from Joe that evening and get his opinion on what could be done about it.

As soon as I had said my goodbyes to Joe, I rang Charles. It took me several attempts to get through to him but, when he finally answered his mobile, I explained that Joe had got the distinct impression from Patrick that Mark was paying Tessa to make her allegations. Charles, as usual, was very calm and collected in his response to, what I thought was, an explosive development. He advised me to write down exactly what Joe had said while it was fresh in my memory and agreed to meet me the next day to discuss it. I was a bit disappointed by Charles' muted reaction. He didn't seem nearly as excited as I thought he would be, but when I got home I did as he had advised and wrote everything down in my diary. For the first time in a long time I felt that maybe, just maybe, things were moving in my favour and I slept well that night.

—

I got to Charles' building half an hour early the next morning and spent twenty minutes pacing up and down in the reception area before an unsmiling, middle-aged woman appeared and told me to follow her. When we arrived at Charles' office, she knocked on the door and opened it without waiting for a response. Charles was sitting at his at his desk, engrossed in paperwork. He glanced up and then leapt to his feet as soon as he saw it was me. He diverted me away from his desk to a little area in the corner of his office where a leather armchair and a double-seated, leather sofa were arranged around a coffee table. He didn't bother with any small talk and asked me straight away what I had discovered. I started with a preamble to the conversation I had with Joe the previous evening.

"Well, you know that I have always believed that Mark is behind what both Rosie and Tessa are claiming?"

"Yes."

"I think that Rosie has been bullied into doing exactly what Mark wants her to do. He wants her to claim that I raped her just because he can't stand the fact that she has been unfaithful to him and, worse still, that she has been unfaithful with me."

Charles looked straight at me and said, with just a touch of exasperation in his voice, "Tom I know very well what your theories are and I believe that you are innocent, but if you could cut to the chase that would be very useful. Tell me what you found out last night and from whom."

"Yes, of course. Sorry… I'll get on with it."

I related as accurately as I possibly could what Joe had told me, whilst frequently referring to my diary to make sure I left nothing out. When I had finished Charles leant forward in his chair, stroked his chin and grimaced before saying, "So, at no point did Patrick actually say that Mark had paid Tessa. It was Joe that came to that conclusion."

I paused for a while before replying and thought to myself that, as usual, Charles had analysed the situation perfectly. Even to me, this didn't sound as big a development as I had thought the previous evening, but I wasn't about to give up on it just yet.

"Look, I can see what you're getting at. I know that it was Joe's theory that Mark must have paid Tessa to make her allegations and I know that, at best, Patrick was just hinting at Mark having 'sorted things out', but I see this as my only hope."

"What do you mean?"

"I mean that I believe Joe's theory that Mark has paid Tessa to come forward. I believe it because I *have* to believe it and I want somehow to prove it because, if I don't, then I also believe there's a good chance I'll go to prison." I left this statement hanging in the air for a while before continuing, "Are there people out there that I can hire to try and prove my theory? You know, a private investigator or a private detective or something?"

After a pause, Charles said, "Yes, I do know people that do that sort of thing."

"Are they the sort of people who can carry out a financial investigation as well as just visually monitoring their subject? If Mark has paid Tessa to make this allegation, he will be clever about it. He won't just have transferred the money into her bank account, he will have done it in a way that he thinks is undetectable. I would need someone who can both physically monitor Tessa to see if there are unusual spending patterns, and be able to carry out a financial investigation to trace any transfer of funds from Mark to Tessa, however sophisticated or complex the transfer is."

"You've obviously given this some thought."

"The way I see it, the most likely way – possibly the

only way – for me to avoid being found guilty is to prove that Mark has paid Tessa. So yes, I have given it a lot of thought."

Charles was silent for a considerable amount of time. He sat with his legs crossed stroking his chin. I was on the verge of speaking a couple of times, but I decided to stay quiet and wait for him to speak first. After what seemed an interminable wait, Charles cleared his throat and began.

"I know exactly the right man for this job. He is ex-forces – I think he worked for the Intelligence Corp – and he works with a team of associates. But, you need to understand a number of things before I approach him. Firstly, this will be very expensive."

"How expensive?"

"That all depends on how much time you want him to spend searching for the evidence we need. The best thing to do is for me to arrange a meeting between the three of us, during which, you can describe your suspicions. He will no doubt ask a number of questions and then he will come back to me with a quote for an initial investigation. It will be thousands of pounds. If you decide, after that initial period of investigation, that it's worth continuing, then the final bill could be tens of thousands."

"I'll have to discuss this with Jilly, but I'm confident that she'll agree. I can't see that there's any alternative."

"The other thing you need to understand, Tom, is that most of these investigations are, in my experience, unsuccessful and they are unsuccessful for a number of reasons."

"Such as?"

"Well, the main reason that evidence is not found is that there isn't any to find in the first place. In this case, it seems to me that you are proceeding on the basis of your friend Joe's suspicions. He doesn't have any evidence that Mark has paid Tessa. He just *thinks* that's what happened. He may well be wrong, and if he is, then there is no evidence to find."

"But I think that Joe is right. I think that Mark *has* paid Tessa."

"Okay. Well, let's assume for a moment that you're correct. That doesn't mean that our detective will find any evidence. It is quite likely, even if there has been some wrongdoing, that it will have been covered up well enough for it to be impossible to get any proof. In addition to this, even if there is some evidence of wrongdoing, that evidence may well be circumstantial in which case it either can't be used in court or it can't be used to worthwhile effect."

"Bloody hell Charles, you really are a bundle of hope and optimism aren't you?"

"All I'm trying to do is manage your expectations, Tom. I don't want you thinking that this is likely to work. It isn't, and it would be wrong of me to advise you to the contrary."

"I understand, but I still think it's worth a try. How quickly can you arrange a meeting with this guy?"

"I will call him this afternoon and get a meeting set up as soon as possible."

Despite Charles' downbeat appraisal of the probability of success, I still felt better having given him the instruction to arrange a meeting. According to him, there was little prospect of success, but at least I was doing something, and that had to be better than doing nothing.

# Chapter 20

## *Magistrates' Court*

A couple of days after deciding to go ahead with hiring a private detective, I found myself in the magistrates' court. I had been calm in the run up to the day, because Charles had reassured me over and over again that this was just a straightforward process whereby the case would be sent to the Crown Court for a preliminary hearing. I, in turn, had tried to re-assure Jilly that there was nothing to worry about, but she wasn't easily convinced. She had become so stressed that she had to take a couple of days off work. I tried to be strong for her, and was as patient as possible as she asked the same questions over and over again. She repeatedly grilled me about what had happened with Tessa and Rosie. She also went over and over every detail of my meetings with Charles and did the same with regard to the likely legal process involved with my sort of case.

Because the magistrates' court that I was required to attend was in Wiltshire, Charles and I travelled down the night before. It was only when we arrived at the hotel we'd booked for the duration that I became as worried as Jilly had been for the last few days. I suppose I had been subconsciously harbouring hopes that the police would realise that this was all a terrible mistake and that I would never actually have to go to court. It was obvious to me now that my hopes had been dashed. This was really happening and I was horrified all over again.

The Ship Hotel was an old coaching inn in a market town about five miles from Westbury Magistrates' Court. It looked to me as if it had been built in Tudor times and, when I read the information in my room, this was confirmed. While the current building dated from the sixteenth century, it was claimed in the literature that a coaching inn had existed on the site since the twelfth century. My bedroom, on the other hand, looked like it had been last decorated in the eighties. It wasn't so much shabby-chic as just shabby and dated. I threw my bags onto the oversoft bed and headed downstairs to the restaurant where I found Charles already seated at a table, looking at the menu. Under normal circumstances, Charles and I would have laughed at the fact that the menu looked as if it had last been updated in the same year as my bedroom, but neither of us passed any comment. We ordered a bottle of red wine and two steaks and then I began to confirm with Charles what I could expect to happen the next day and in the months to follow. This was ground that Charles and I had gone over many times in the last couple of months, but it seemed the only sensible thing to be talking about the night before my first visit to court.

The first thing I wanted to check with Charles was, assuming that the allegations were not withdrawn, when I could expect the trial to take place. He explained, once again, that because there was not a great deal of evidence to gather for either the defence or the prosecution that the major factor was the availability of court time. This meant that once the case was referred by the magistrates' court to the Crown Court that it was likely to be at least six months before the case went to trial. He added that it wouldn't be unheard of for there to be a twelve-month wait. The thought of nothing being resolved for twelve months was an excruciating one. My life was going to go on hold for anything up to a year and there was absolutely nothing I could do about it.

After the depressing subject of timescales, we moved on to talking about the barrister who would defend me. Charles was in charge of my defence, but obviously a crucial part of the 'team' was going to be the barrister who would act on my behalf in court. Charles had suggested a guy that he had used on many of his recent high profile cases. He told me that Fergus Pickard was the best defence barrister he had worked with and that, while he wouldn't be cheap, he would be worth every penny of his fee. I realised that we hadn't actually discussed in any detail what the total bill for my defence was likely to be. I took the view that whatever the cost, it was worth it. I knew that Charles would keep his own costs as low as possible, but equally I knew that the private detective and Fergus Pickard, both of whom I was due to meet the next week, would be expensive.

Jilly and I had very little in the way of savings and, therefore, I had concluded that we would probably have to remortgage the house to fund my defence. I had decided that I would have this discussion with Jilly once I had met my defence team and had a better idea of what the actual costs might be. It was not a conversation I was particularly looking forward to.

The one subject I had avoided speaking to Charles about up until this time, was how long I could expect to spend in jail if I was found guilty. I suppose I had avoided the subject because I had been hoping that somehow the police or the CPS would decide that there was no case for me to answer. I was also frightened of the answer that Charles might give me. Now, the night before my first appearance in court, I could avoid reality no longer. It was going to trial and I faced the possibility of being found guilty and serving a lengthy prison sentence.

Nervously I asked, "If the worst comes to the worst and I am found guilty, how long am I likely to go to prison for?"

Charles had obviously done his research and had been anticipating the question. He answered with no hesitation and no visible display of emotion.

"There are relatively new guidelines for offences sentenced on or after the 14th May 2007. For a single offence of rape by a single offender, where the victim is sixteen or over, the usual starting point is five years custody. That is what you can expect if you are found guilty on one count. If you are found guilty of rape involving multiple victims, the usual starting point is a sentence of fifteen years custody with a range of thirteen to nineteen years."

Up until that moment, I suppose, I had been in some sort of denial. I obviously knew that I would go to prison if found guilty, but at the back of my mind I thought that maybe I would be sentenced to three or four years. Reality came crashing in. I felt nauseous and started trembling. After a very long pause, I spoke, "So I could be sentenced to nearly twenty years?"

Charles responded in a very matter of fact way, "It is very unlikely that you would receive the maximum term, but if you are found guilty on both counts you will receive a very long sentence. I would like to sugar the pill, but these are the facts. I would imagine that you would probably receive a sentence at the lower end of the scale because there are no real aggravating factors and there may be some mitigation. I know that this doesn't help at the moment, but you also need to remember that, all things being equal, you would probably only serve half of your sentence."

My shock turned to anger. I was angry with myself for getting into this situation. I was angry with Charles for being so matter of fact about something that would ruin my life and the lives of my family. And I was angry with Mark, because I saw him as the real guilty party. I sat, staring at Charles in silence, until I had collected my thoughts.

I decided that I wasn't going to blame myself for acting in a way that countless men had behaved throughout time. I shouldn't have betrayed Jilly, but that was hardly a hanging or, in this case, an imprisonable offence. I very quickly decided that

Charles' lack of emotion and apparently uncaring attitude was the only way he could deliver such unpalatable news. He had probably been dreading the question and had thought that the best way to answer was in as matter of fact a way as possible. That left me being angry with Mark and, to a lesser extent, with Rosie and Tessa. I should have perhaps been just as angry with Rosie and Tessa, but I knew, in my heart, that Mark was the one who was driving the whole situation. Shock had turned to anger which had turned to hatred. It all came flowing out through my tightly gritted teeth.

"I fucking hate that bastard. I really fucking hate him."

Charles reached out, touched me on the arm and said quietly, "Okay, Tom. Calm down."

With my teeth still gritted, I slammed my fist into the table, "Fuck calming down! He's caused all of this. He couldn't fucking bear me having sex with Rosie and so he's trying to destroy me. I could go to prison for ten years just because that bastard can't bear losing to me at anything."

Charles tried, again, to calm me down, "Look Tom, I know you're angry but this isn't going to help. We've all got to stay focused on what we can do before this goes to trial – if indeed it does go to trial – to give you the best chance."

"What do you mean *if* it goes to trial? Of course it's going to go to fucking trial."

"You shouldn't think that it is a certainty that there will be a trial. There are any number of reasons that it might not."

"Such as?"

"Well, either one, or both of your accusers could refuse to give evidence in court. It may be that information comes to the attention of the prosecution, which completely undermines the credibility of our accusers. It may be that our P.I. uncovers this information or that it comes from a source that we don't know about yet. At the risk of repeating myself, you should hope for the best and plan for the worst. What you must do is stay calm and make sure that you give the best assistance you can to your barrister when you meet him next week."

I did manage to calm down at this stage and have a much more sensible conversation with Charles. He emphasised, once again, that there was still a possibility that I wouldn't have to face trial, but that I certainly shouldn't put too much faith in this outcome. He mostly stressed the crucial importance of the credibility, in front of a jury, of my accusers and, of course, of me. I went up to my room in quite an optimistic mood. I convinced myself that the P.I. would be able to, either uncover evidence of Mark having paid Tessa to come forward, or at least to come up with information that undermined her character. It was much more difficult for me to think how Rosie's integrity or character could be questioned. She had, as far as I knew, lived a blameless life and was now a very respectable wife, mother and charity fundraiser.

I had to remind myself that although she was completely dominated by Mark, she was the one who seemed set on giving evidence against me in court and that this evidence could help to convict me and condemn me to years in prison. I was determined that from that moment on I would consider her just as guilty as Mark of conspiring against me. She was a grown woman who was responsible for her own decisions. It occurred to me, however, that if she had become so beaten down over the years by Mark that she was no longer responsible for her own actions, then maybe her credibility could be called into question. I went to sleep content that there was at least some hope for me.

My visit to Westbury Magistrates' Court passed in a blur. Charles had assured me over and over again that it was pure 'process'. A case as serious as mine could not be tried in a magistrates' court and therefore it was just a matter of going through the procedure of referring it to the Crown Court. However, despite Charles' assurances, I was terrified as I entered the court. Maybe it was the fact that I'd never been in any sort of court before and it was the fear of the unknown, but I had all sorts of things going through my head. I was worried I'd say something stupid or incriminating, or that they would decide I should be kept in custody until the trial or that I'd be accused of something else. Thankfully, before I could become too hysterical, it was all over. I did little more than confirm my name and address before it was announced that the case would be heard at Crown Court and the date was set for the preliminary hearing. Although I was relieved as Charles and I left the magistrates' court, it also occurred to me that Jilly, the boys and me would have a pretty miserable Christmas. It was the 2nd of December and in a normal month I could have expected my first Crown Court date to be in about three weeks time, but specifically because we were approaching the Christmas period, the date was set for the 15th of January. I had another interminable wait of six weeks to look forward to.

# Chapter 21

## *Meeting the defence team*

Harry Sharples was not what I expected. I had a clear vision in my mind of what an ex-Intelligence Corp, private investigator, would look like. I had imagined an angular, sharp-suited, suave ex-public schoolboy. What I got, could only be described as a shambling mess. He was twenty minutes late for our meeting, which was held at Charles' office, and when he eventually arrived he offered nothing in the way of an apology. He was short, fat and bald, and the little bit of hair that he did have was overlong and hung, limply, at either side of his head. When Charles introduced us, Sharples offered me a weak, slightly damp handshake. I had been hoping to be introduced to someone who inspired me with confidence, but my first impressions were not good. To compound my disappointment, Sharples hadn't even bothered to wear a suit. He wore cheap acrylic trousers and a shapeless patterned jumper over a shirt with a frayed collar.

As the three of us settled down around the coffee table in Charles' office, I decided that I must be more positive. I told myself that it didn't matter what he looked like, the only important thing was the expertise he could bring to bear on my upcoming trial. Charles spoke first and, after explaining that he had provided Sharples with an outline of the case, asked me to tell him what I wanted to achieve by hiring a private detective.

I started off by emphasising that I was completely innocent of all the charges. I wasn't sure whether this made any difference to the dishevelled man sitting opposite me, but I felt better for saying it. I explained that I thought Mark was motivated by an unquenchable desire to win at everything he did and that the 'loss' of Rosie to me, however temporary, would have enraged and humiliated him. I described what I saw as the cruel and abusive relationship he had with Rosie, and said that I believed that he had bullied her into making her accusation. I made special mention of the fact that I thought he would do anything to get revenge on me. I realised that none of this was directly relevant to uncovering what Mark had done to persuade Tessa to make her accusation. It was, in fact, completely irrelevant, but I wanted him to be motivated not just by the money that I was paying him, but by a sense of justice.

Sharples had taken a biro and a notebook out of his back pocket just before I had started talking, but up until this point he hadn't written anything down. As soon as I started talking about Tessa's accusation however, he picked up his pen and started writing. Two things immediately occurred to me. Firstly, that Charles must have already briefed him as to what he would be specifically investigating, and secondly, that he was motivated by the fee he would be receiving, as opposed to anything more altruistic. I looked at this positively and came to the conclusion that this sort of approach indicated that I was dealing with a professional. I decided to be reassured. When Sharples started talking,

I was even more reassured. In a very matter of fact way he told me that I should refer to him as Harry and that he would be calling me Tom. He didn't wait for me to agree before telling me that he didn't need any further background on what had happened between Tessa and me thirty years previously. He only wanted to know why I thought that Mark had paid her to make her accusations and whether I had any evidence to back my theory up. He might not have looked like I thought he would, but Sharples certainly met my expectations when it came to his approach.

After I had finished relaying my theory, Sharples sat in silence for a short time while he read through the notes he'd made. This gave me a chance to consider just what evidence there was to indicate Mark had paid Tessa and how strong that evidence was. I suddenly had this terrible feeling that I was clutching at straws. In essence, I suspected Mark had paid Tessa because he had a history of getting exactly what he wanted by paying for it. My, perhaps tenuous, suspicions had then been confirmed by a man, Joe Donnelly, who hated Mark and had interpreted a fairly innocuous comment as proof that a payment had been made to Tessa.

I was half expecting Sharples to comment in a derogatory way about the strength of my theory and the evidence to support it, but that's not what he did. He simply told me what he proposed to do. He would carry out some background checks to find out whether Tessa had a criminal record or had, at any time during the last thirty years, been in trouble with the police. He would also check to see if she had a history of being in debt and, if relevant, whether these debts were owed to legitimate or illegitimate bodies. Further checks would be made into any personal relationships Tessa had been involved in since I'd last seen her and whether any of the people she'd been involved with had criminal records. Sharples also mentioned ascertaining whether social services had ever had any dealings with her or her family. He went on to say that he would also utilise social and business networking sites to build up a picture of Tessa and how she lived her life. I didn't actually know what he meant by this. He explained that if she had a presence for example on Facebook, MySpace or LinkedIn then he could use that information to help build a profile of Tessa. Sharples' use of the Internet to build a profile seemed, at the time, to be incredibly sophisticated.

I had wanted to interrupt Sharples on several occasions to ask him how he intended to access these various sources of information. It occurred to me that at least some of these sources were not available to anyone else other than the appropriate authorities. I stopped myself because of the specific instructions that Charles had given me just before Sharples had arrived at his offices. Charles had explained that we were to assume that his methods were completely legitimate and that, as long as we didn't know of any wrongdoing, then we would not be compromised in any way. When I asked Charles whether information gained through 'suspect' methods would be inadmissible in a court of law, he said I'd been watching too many American films. He stressed that we should gather the evidence first and then worry about its "admissibility" later. He assured me that there was usually a way of working this type of evidence into a case. With this in mind, I sat in silence as Sharples went on to describe the second part of his plan of action. He spoke of "physical and financial surveillance" and of "changes in patterns of behaviour" as well as utilising his associates' "forensic accounting expertise." When he had finished, I was left with two very conflicting impressions. One was of a man who understood what I wanted from him and was going to do a thorough and professional job. The other wasn't too different from my first impression of Harry Sharples. He looked like a seedy, little man and he was going to employ pretty seedy methods to try and achieve his goals.

Once he had left, Charles declared that he thought that Sharples had properly grasped the two very distinct elements of his brief. I didn't immediately understand what Charles meant by this. As far as I was concerned there was only one thing that Sharples needed to do, and that was to prove that Mark had paid Tessa to accuse me of rape. Charles came straight to the point in setting me straight.

"That would obviously be the ideal scenario but, as I've said before, we've got to plan for the worst, and the worst scenario is that we find absolutely no evidence of any payment from Mark to Tessa. If that is the case then we're left with trying to undermine Tessa's credibility in the eyes of the jury."

"So you don't think we'll find any evidence of a payment?"

"I'm not saying that, but there is a possibility that no payment was ever made. If that is the case then no matter how good Sharples is – and in my opinion he's very good – he won't find evidence of a payment because there wasn't one."

"Well, I'm stuffed if that's the case."

"Not necessarily, and that's the point I'm making. The first part of his brief is to uncover evidence of a payment. If he manages to do that then things are looking very good for you. If he doesn't, then the second part of his brief comes into play, and that is to find out any information about Tessa that would undermine her in the eyes of the jury."

"What sort of information do you mean?"

"It could be anything. Maybe she has been in trouble with the police before, or she's got a drink problem, or money problems or she's made false accusations before. Essentially anything that would reduce her credibility."

—

On my way home from Charles' office I reflected on the meeting. Despite my initial impression, I was hopeful that Sharples would do a good job. I was optimistic in terms of him being able to uncover something about either Tessa or Mark that would help my case. It was obvious, although he hadn't said it, that Charles thought that the most likely way in which Sharples could help us, would be to concentrate on Tessa's credibility as a witness. But he didn't know Mark like I knew Mark. I was still confident that he had done more than just use his powers of persuasion to encourage Tessa to come forward. Mark believed that all problems could be solved by throwing money at them and I was convinced that he had thrown money at this problem. I was less convinced that Sharples would find evidence of this. Mark was no fool and I knew that if he *had* paid Tessa, he would have worked out a way of doing it, which was difficult – if not impossible – to detect.

As I approached home, my mind turned to Jilly. She had been suffering very badly since I had been charged with the second offence. She had missed a lot of work and had been to see the doctor on several occasions. He had diagnosed her as suffering from anxiety and depression, and had prescribed a fairly high dose of something called mirtazapine. I felt a mixture of surprise and frustration. Surprise because Jilly had always seemed so strong, both mentally and physically. I was frustrated for a number of different reasons. My frustration stemmed from the fact that I wasn't able to comfort Jilly. When she cried and I went to put my arm around her, she moved away from me. After my appearance at the magistrates' court, whenever I tried to talk to her, she would clam up and make it clear that she didn't want to discuss anything with me. I was also frustrated because I had to shoulder the burden of this dreadful situation by myself. Jilly, who had always portrayed herself to the outside world as the strong one in our relationship, had, when it really mattered, proven herself to be the weak one.

When I got home, Jilly was lying on the sofa in the sitting room. She was looking pale and thin. She managed a half smile as I came into the room and, despite her recent reluctance to talk to me, she asked how my meeting had gone. I decided to keep my answer as brief and as positive as possible.

"Yeah, it was good. The private detective, a chap called Harry Sharples, wasn't exactly what I expected but he was very professional and I think he'll do a good job."

Jilly managed another weak smile, but her response was even briefer than mine, "Oh good, I'm pleased."

I thought about going into more detail, but decided that it was probably best not to. Jilly just didn't look as if she could cope with another conversation about my case, so I offered her a cup of tea and when she accepted I wandered off into the kitchen. When I came back into the sitting room she didn't ask any more questions and I took this as a clear indication that I should talk about something else.

In one sense, I was quite relieved that Jilly didn't seem either willing or able to talk in any detail about my case. There was one subject in particular that I was very glad to avoid and that was the subject of money. Jilly and I had discussed the cost of my defence shortly after I had been arrested for the first time, but not since. At that stage, Charles had explained that his costs and the costs of any barrister employed would vary depending upon whether the case went to trial. If it didn't go to trial, then the cost would be limited to his charges, which could amount to less than ten thousand pounds. If it did, then the costs for him and the barrister combined would be several tens of thousands of pounds. I had been deliberately vague when I discussed this with Jilly and had stressed that it was still possible that the CPS may decide not to prosecute.

Charles had explained in more detail, just prior to our meeting with Sharples, what a trial was likely to mean in terms of specific costs. His own fees would be around fifty thousand pounds, as would those of my barrister. In addition to this, he estimated that the services of Sharples were likely to be between ten and twenty thousand pounds. As I looked at the wan face of my depressed and vulnerable wife, I knew that now was not the time to reveal that the trial that I faced would probably cost us over a hundred thousand pounds. I had already paid deposits to Charles and Sharples and I had no idea how I was going to find the rest of the money without remortgaging our house. All I knew was that, whatever the cost, I was willing to pay it. This wasn't a matter of life and death, but if I were found guilty, my life and probably those of Jilly and the boys would be ruined. For the foreseeable future, at least, the burden of the potentially huge cost of my defence was something that I would have to shoulder alone.

To my surprise, and I have to say relief, Jilly went back to work the next day. I was due to meet my barrister for the first time at the end of the week and I felt better able to prepare for this meeting without having to look after Jilly. Not that there was actually much preparation to be done because, at this stage, all I would be required to do was to give my side of the story once again. I would be repeating exactly what I had told Charles and, of course, the police. After Jilly had gone to work that Thursday morning, I went through, with the help of my diary, the sequence of events that had led to me having sex with both Tessa and Rosie. I crosschecked everything I could remember with what I had written in my diary. There wasn't really too much to it and I ended up spending much of the day watching TV and getting bored. I had plenty of time to contemplate how much I was dreading the five weeks that would separate my initial meetings with my private detective and barrister and my first appearance in Crown Court. Apart from the meetings with my defence team, I wasn't sure what on earth I was going to do with myself.

After a day and a half of doing nothing much, I was relieved, on that Friday afternoon, to finally meet the barrister that Charles had recommended to defend me. Once again, the meeting was held at Charles' office and my first impressions of Fergus Pickard were that he was everything that Harry Sharples was not. He was punctual, smartly dressed in a dark blue suit, and charming from the start. In fact, with his full head of dark brown hair, even features and slim physique, he was almost too perfect. He and Charles had worked together on a number of high profile cases and were obviously very relaxed in each other's company. I, on the other hand, felt very ill at ease. Maybe I was intimidated by the suave and ferociously intelligent Fergus Pickard, or maybe it was the realisation that meeting him meant that my day of reckoning was getting ever closer. Either way, I felt very nervous and it occurred to me that if I felt this way now, what on earth would I feel like when confronted by the prosecution barrister.

Fergus tried his best to relax me. He explained that this was just an introductory meeting and that the main purpose of it was just to get to know each other and to begin the process of constructing a defence. He emphasised that, if there was to be a trial, it was almost certainly some months away and that we had plenty of time to get things right. His manner was both reassuring and confident, and slowly my nervousness dissipated. He told me that he had read through the file that Charles had prepared for him, but that he wanted to go through, with me, exactly what had happened with Tessa and Rosie. I presumed that this was to make sure that there were no relevant differences between what I had told Charles and the police during my interviews, and my current version of events. I realised that Fergus had probably represented clients whose version of events changed every time they recounted them and he was already assessing what sort of client I was going to be. I was confident that there would be no such discrepancies in my case. My confidence was based on the simplicity of my version of events and the fact that I had read through my diary several times in preparation for this meeting.

Having listened intently to me for an hour or so, Fergus then outlined how he planned to build a defence case. He reiterated what Charles had already told me. The key to the trial would be the credibility of the various witnesses, in the eyes of the jury.. He wanted to know whether there was anything in my past that the prosecution could use to undermine my credibility. He was particularly interested in the staff at the Cottage who had seen how Rosie and I had interacted during the run up to the alleged rape. On the subject of Rosie, he asked me to go away and think about whether there was anything in her past that could be seen as detrimental to her character. He encouraged me to speak to anybody who might know more about her than I did. Fergus asked me if he could liaise with Sharples before he started his investigation of Tessa. He wanted to make sure that Sharples would be looking for all the things that could be useful to my defence. At the end of the meeting, I was confident that Charles had appointed a barrister who would leave nothing to chance.

When I left the meeting, I was once again feeling optimistic. My meetings with both Fergus Pickard and Harry Sharples had gone well, and I was happy that the defence team that Charles had assembled was going to give me the best possible chance of proving my innocence. I was desperate for a beer but my options, in terms of drinking partners, were pretty limited. I didn't think it was a good idea to suggest to Charles and Fergus that we all go for a drink. I'm sure they would have politely declined if I had asked them. I couldn't ask any of my colleagues at work as they had probably been told that I would be absent for some time. My regular drinking mates at The Red Lion had probably found out what the real reason for Mark's attack on me had been, and I didn't relish the prospect of answering any questions from them. That left me with only one real option... Joe Donnelly. I didn't really fancy his company, but he was the only person I could think of to have a drink with. I also knew that despite it being a Friday night, he would have no other plans.

# Chapter 22

## *A mixed bag for Christmas*

The next week I got a call from the boys' housemaster. He told me that both Max and Sam had been involved in minor incidents and that he would like Jilly and I to come and see him. I had been taking advantage of my enforced absence from work to go and watch as many of their rugby matches as possible, but I had only spoken to Mr Woodgate briefly on a couple of occasions. I was working on the basis that he would contact us if there were any problems. The boys had been coping in very different ways. Max wanted to be kept informed of every development, whether it be a court date or a meeting with the defence team. Sam, on the other hand, didn't want to talk about it at all. I did my best to give them the impression that everything was under control, but every now and then I would see a look of panic in their faces. I felt terribly guilty at these times.

It was the last Saturday of the Christmas term when Jilly and I met up with Mr Woodgate. He was his usual smiling, enthusiastic self when he ushered us into his study. He reassured us, before we had even sat down, that neither of the boys were in serious trouble, but told us that he was concerned that the deterioration in their behaviour could escalate in the future. Max had been involved in two altercations in the last couple of weeks. The first had taken place on the rugby field. One of

Max's closest friends had tackled him hard, but fairly, during practice. This was something that would have happened countless times over the years. Max's reaction was to lash out at him and a fight had ensued which was quickly broken up by other boys. This was totally out of character for Max. He was undoubtedly a tough player on the rugby pitch, but he had never lashed out at anyone. The rugby coach had not punished Max, but he had reported it to Mr Woodgate because he had been told to keep an eye on him as he was having 'difficulties' at home. The second incident was of much more concern. Max had attacked another boy over a disagreement about what to watch on TV.

My initial reaction to what Mr Woodgate had told me was relief. I had assumed when he first told us about the fights, that Max had reacted to comments made about my arrest. Thankfully, it appeared that the news had not reached the other boys at the school. I felt that it was inevitable that word would get out at some point, but at least it wasn't something we would have to deal with just yet. Max had been punished for the second incident with a number of detentions and it had been decided, with the headmaster, that this would suffice for the time being. Mr Woodgate stressed that any further incidents of this nature would have to be dealt with by a suspension and that Max was aware of this. It was agreed that I would have a word with him and make sure that there were no similar outbursts.

Sam's transgressions were equally out of character, but nowhere near as serious. He had failed to do his homework on a number of occasions and had been sent out of class a couple of times for answering back to his teachers. Sam had, throughout his school life, been a very diligent and well-behaved student, so this behaviour was very surprising to everyone. The fact that Sam was reluctant to talk to anyone about the difficulties at home, made it tricky to work out whether his change in behaviour was due to these difficulties or just a stage he was going through. It was decided that while I was talking to Max, Jilly should have a chat with Sam.

On the way home, Jilly told me that Sam had been very contrite about his behaviour and promised to be a "good boy" for the few remaining days of the term. My chat with Max, on the other hand, could only be described as traumatic. We went for a walk around the school cricket pitch and as soon as I made mention of the two incidents, he burst into tears and became incoherent. I hadn't seen him cry for a good few years and his obvious distress was harrowing. I put my arms around him and held him until his sobs subsided.

As soon as he was calm enough he said, "I'm sorry for causing you these extra problems just when you don't need them, it's just that I get so angry sometimes."

I couldn't believe that he was apologising to me. Whichever way you looked at it, I knew that if I hadn't had sex with Rosie, none of this would have happened. It should have been me apologising to him.

"You don't need to say sorry to me, Max. I just want to make sure you are okay and that you don't get in any more trouble. It might be a stupid question, but what is making you angry?"

"Those two fucking, lying bitches. They're trying to ruin your life just to keep that bastard, Mark, happy."

I hadn't heard Max swear like that before. I was sure that he swore with his friends, but he'd never done it in front of me before. I decided not to comment on it. I was more interested in calming him down and making sure that he kept himself out of trouble.

"Max, I really appreciate your support, but you mustn't let yourself get so wound up. They're winning if you do. You've only got a few days of term left and then it's Christmas. Promise me you'll be good until then."

"I promise."

I could tell that he meant it and so I didn't say any more on the subject. We spent the rest of our walk around the cricket pitch discussing what was happening with my case. I had decided that I would be as open as I could with him on the basis that, while he was too young to have to cope with this sort of worry, he was old enough to understand what was going on. I described my meetings with Fergus Pickard and Harry Sharples, and what they were trying to achieve. I told him what the possible schedule was for my trial and gave him the impression that everything would work out well in the end. I didn't necessarily believe this, but I couldn't see any point in making him more worried than he already was.

Thankfully, there were no more incidents before the end of term and when the boys got home for the

Christmas holidays they both seemed to be reasonably happy. I was pretty certain that things would get more difficult for them in the new year. It was almost inevitable that the rumour mill would be in full flow over the holidays and likely that, when they got back to school, the rumours about me would spread very quickly. Jilly and I realised that we would have to prepare them for this. We also knew that, at some point, Sam would start asking questions, and that for both of them, the possibility of their father going to prison would hit them hard. For the time being however, we decided to make Christmas 2009 as happy and relaxed for the boys as possible.

—

Charles and I had a couple of encouraging meetings with Sharples just prior to Christmas. He had managed to find out an incredible amount of information about Tessa and the life she had lived since leaving her job at St Michael's. Most of the information he gathered pointed towards a very mundane existence. She had worked in a supermarket for a couple of years after she had left, before spending a year working as a waitress in a coffee shop. After this, she had trained as a secretary and then started working at R.J. Grimwade, a company based in Surrey, which manufactured and sold air-conditioning units. Since leaving St. Michael's she didn't appear to have had any meaningful relationships, or indeed any boyfriends at all, until she started dating Chris Scobell who was an engineer at R.J.

Grimwade. By this time, she was in her early twenties. During this whole period, she had lived at home with her mother in Surrey. She had no criminal record and, apart from being caught speeding in 1985, she had never had any dealings with the police.

Tessa and her boyfriend, Chris, had moved into rented accommodation, close to where they worked, when she was twenty-four. They remained in their rented flat for a couple of years before being re-located to Grimwade's office in Gloucestershire two years later. In 1992 they bought their first home together. It was a three bedroomed, end of terrace house costing thirty-two thousand pounds. The house had formally been a council property. Tessa and Chris had got married in October 1994 and their first child, a boy called Nathan, had been born in February 1995. Their second child, Karen, had been born two years later. In June 2008, R.J. Grimwade had made thirty percent of their workforce redundant and both Tessa and Chris had lost their jobs. Within three months she had managed to find another full-time job as a receptionist at a local solicitors, but Chris had not been so lucky. He had found temporary work at a number of local firms doing a variety of unskilled jobs. None of these jobs had lasted for more than a couple of months and all were poorly paid. He had not worked at all for the last six weeks.

As of December 2009 they were still living in the same house. It was valued at approximately one hundred and ten thousand pounds. The original mortgage on the property had been twenty-five thousand pounds, but Tessa and Chris had remortgaged the property twice, the last time being 2006. The current mortgage stood at eighty-seven thousand pounds. According to Sharples, they had never been behind on their mortgage payments until they lost their jobs at Grimwade's. They were currently three months behind on their payments, but as recently as October of 2009 they had been six months in arrears.

This last point was of great interest to me. I couldn't see how, with Chris still out of work, they had managed to reduce their mortgage arrears from six to three months. Some of their other debts had also been reduced in the last couple of months. For example, their overdraft, which had been running at one thousand pounds in October, was now at zero. I asked Sharples whether there had been any evidence of extra money being paid into their account. He told me that although no extra funds had been paid into the account, expenditure from it, had slowed markedly. Apart from standing orders and direct debits, which obviously had to be paid from their bank account, there had been virtually no other withdrawals. When I suggested to Sharples that Tessa must be receiving cash from somewhere and that it was probably coming from Mark, he said that he had "not managed to prove either of these things at this stage."

I was a bit disappointed at Sharples' decidedly lukewarm reaction to my suggestion that Tessa was living on cash supplied to her by Mark. However, my initial disappointment was quickly eased by his plans for the next part of his investigation. In the immediate run up to, and over the Christmas period, Sharples planned to put Tessa and her immediate family under surveillance. This, he told me, meant that he and his colleagues would be able to confirm whether she was handling suspicious amounts of cash. He went on to say that any additional cash could have come from any number of different sources and that it was unlikely that physical surveillance alone would reveal what this source was. He intended to continue, what he referred to as, his "electronic and digital" surveillance, as this was more likely to reveal whether Mark was the source of any extra funds.

Just before we parted company, I asked him if I could have a copy of the report that he had read from during our meeting. As diplomatically as possible, he declined my request, hinting at the fact that much of the information he had gathered was not in the public domain and therefore that his reports were going to remain in his possession. When Charles abruptly brought the meeting to a close, I understood that I should not have made this request. Once Sharples had left, Charles reiterated that we should not ask where he got his information from, rather we should just assume that it was collected legally.

"If we don't ask questions about the sources of his information," he explained, "then we won't get any answers that we don't like." For this same reason, I didn't ask Charles for his opinion on what Sharples had found out about Tessa. I knew that he would basically say that, while the information Sharples had provided was very detailed, it didn't actually prove anything. I wanted to get to Christmas in as positive a mind-set as possible and that meant being optimistic about Sharples' research. He had found out that Tessa had money difficulties and that, with no obvious source of extra cash, she was paying off her debts. That gave me hope that my theory about Mark paying Tessa could still be true and *that*, at this stage, was something I wanted to hold on to.

—

Christmas 2009 was, bearing in mind the circumstances, a pretty decent time for the Bishop family. The pills that Jilly had been prescribed seemed to be having a positive effect and she was definitely in better spirits than she'd been a couple of weeks earlier. The boys had kept out of trouble in their last few days at school before the holidays and had been busy with friends since they broke up. I spoke to them separately just before Christmas Day to make sure they were coping. Sam didn't really want to talk about anything, but he listened when I said that I had a great defence team and that things were looking positive. Max wanted to know more detail, but I basically told him the same as I had told Sam. I was very aware that although he thought he was grown up, he was only sixteen and I didn't want to overburden him. Both of them hugged me once our conversations had ended.

My father arrived at our house on Christmas Eve

afternoon, and from then, until New Year, none of us talked about my upcoming trial. We went for drinks that evening at a neighbour's house. I was always worried that, wherever I went, somebody would know what I'd been accused of and judge me. Thankfully, although we were very friendly with some of them, we had always kept our neighbours separate from our other friends. I could tell from their reaction to me that none of them had a clue what was going on in my life and I was able to completely relax.

Christmas Day was no different from the ones that the five of us had enjoyed since my mother's death five years earlier. The boys woke Jilly and I up very early and, once my father had been roused, we spent a couple of hours in our pyjamas opening presents. I then cooked a full English breakfast, which we ate while still in our pyjamas. We all ate far too much. After breakfast, we washed and then dressed in as many 'Christmassy' jumpers, hats and scarves as we could find before walking the couple of hundred yards to the local church. The boys obviously attended church services at school but this was the one annual trip that Jilly and I made. After church, it was back home for champagne and smoked salmon. Jilly then stayed at home preparing lunch while the rest of us went on a long walk or, as the boys referred to it, a "forced march." We were back in time for the Queen's Speech and, as soon as it was over, we tucked into our Christmas lunch. After lunch, I dozed in my armchair like an old man for an hour or so until Sam woke me up and demanded that we played games. We argued good-naturedly throughout every game that we played, watched some crap TV and then went to bed. We had a lovely time, and it was the first day since I had been arrested that I had not, at some point, felt sick with fear.

Boxing day was not such a good day. The four of us spent the day at Jilly's parents along with her sister, Claire, and Claire's husband, Toby. My father had been invited, but just as he had done for the previous few years he came up with an excuse as to why he wouldn't be able to make it. This excuse was for Jilly's benefit as he didn't want to upset her, but he had told me a couple of years previously that he would rather spend Boxing day "alone, than with that woman." "That woman" referred to Jilly's mother, Anne. Most people tried to avoid her as much as possible, but through a sense of duty, there was no avoiding her at Christmas. We spent a thoroughly unpleasant few hours in her company.

Anne's behaviour that day was fairly typical. Just before lunch, Toby and I got stuck with her in the kitchen. She talked, without drawing breath, about herself and the minutiae of her life for a good twenty minutes. I knew that the wisest tactic was just to nod occasionally, try and ignore what she was saying and then move away as soon as possible. Toby was not so wise. About ten minutes into her diatribe, he made the mistake of interrupting her to ask a question. Anne thrust her head towards him and shouted at him to "stop interrupting me" and then accused him of being a "very rude man." There was real anger in her voice.

Over lunch, Anne berated Jilly for not coming to see her more often. When Jilly apologised and explained that she was very busy at work, Anne dismissed her career as a "silly little job." Anne then claimed that Jilly was being a neglectful mother for even going to work and then insulted me for not earning enough to support my family properly. She then turned her attention to Claire. She accused Claire of being ungrateful because she couldn't immediately remember what present she had given her for Christmas. Anne seemed obsessed with everybody agreeing that her present was the perfect gift. She, of course, was quite happy to dismiss a gift given to her as "something I've already got" or "the wrong colour."

Jilly's father, John, was the polar opposite of her mother. He'd had a very successful business career, was loved and adored by his daughters and admired by everyone that met him. I had always enjoyed his company and would have definitely spent more time with him if it hadn't meant spending more time with Anne. He was a great conversationalist, genuinely interested in other people and was disarmingly modest. There were only two things about John that mystified me. Firstly, why on earth had he married Anne and secondly, why he had stayed married to her? To be fair to him, until recently, he had always managed to control the worst of Anne's outbursts with a mixture of charm and wit. Sadly, now that his physical and mental health was on the wane, he was no longer able to do this. That made things worse for everybody else, but what was really upsetting was that Anne was beginning to treat him badly. Increasingly, she would shout him down when he disagreed with her and blame their lack of a social life on his lack of physical mobility. In short, as he became more reliant upon her, she was tormenting him. Jilly and Claire often jumped to their father's defence if Anne was criticising or haranguing him, but it didn't seem to have any impact on her behaviour.

After lunch, Toby and I volunteered to do the washing up so that we could keep away from Anne who had set up court in the sitting room. We didn't exactly talk directly about her, but when Toby asked me, "What excuse have you come up with to leave early?" we both knew exactly what he meant.

By half past four, Jilly and I had made our excuses and we were on our way home with the boys. I felt guilty about leaving early, but not because of the fuss made by Anne about hardly ever seeing us. I felt guilty because John was stuck with her and had no chance of escape. It was the only time that day that I thought about what the future held for me. My, only slightly tongue-in-cheek, thought was that although I could be facing prison in the new year, I would prefer that type of prison to the one that John faced for the rest of his life.

# Chapter 23

## *Reality*

I had my first meeting of 2010 with Sharples, in early January. I don't know whether he had a family, but it was obvious that if he did, he hadn't spent much time with them over the festive period. He had done most of the "physical surveillance" of Tessa himself and had taken photographs and made voice recordings of her every day from the middle of December until after New Year. This included Christmas Day itself. Sharples had evidence that proved that Tessa had spent relatively large amounts of money buying presents, drinks, cinema tickets and large electrical items both before and after Christmas. All of her purchases had been made in cash. Her bank statement also showed that her mortgage arrears and other debts had reduced further. Sharples reported all of this in a very matter of fact and calm way, but I could tell he was very pleased with himself. His tone of voice indicated to me that he felt that he had done a good job and I agreed with him. As far as I was concerned, this was the breakthrough that I was looking for. The money had to be coming from somewhere or somebody, and I was convinced that 'somebody' was Mark.

While I was getting excited, Charles introduced his own bit of reality into the situation by asking whether there was any evidence to suggest where this money was coming from. Sharples was very straightforward in his response. There was no evidence that money had been paid into any bank accounts held by Tessa, or her husband, from an unusual source. In addition to this, he told us that he had not witnessed anybody giving Tessa or Chris any cash. He emphasised that neither of them had made mention of extra cash in any of the conversations he and his colleagues had directly overheard, or during conversations that they'd had over their mobile and landlines. His last statement immediately got me thinking. I was intrigued as to how on earth was he able to listen in on mobile and landline conversations. Charles had drummed into me that we didn't need or want to know how he obtained his information and so, despite my curiosity, I didn't ask any questions.

Before Sharples left, I congratulated him on his success and told him to keep up the good work. I was feeling a lot more upbeat than I had in a while. The way I looked at it, the more evidence of unusual spending patterns, the better. I was convinced Mark was behind Tessa and Chris' improved financial position and was confident that if anyone could find the link to Mark, then it would be Sharples. Even without a link being established, I was sure that if Tessa kept spending and her financial position kept improving then that could be used in court to undermine her credibility. If she couldn't account for the money then surely this would raise the suspicions of the jury. As soon as Sharples had left the room I shared my optimism with Charles.

"He's doing a great job. I'm sure he's going to get the information we need to prove that Mark is bankrolling Tessa," I said.

Charles' response was, yet again, not what I was hoping for, "Hold on a minute Tom, I think you need to slow down a bit. Yes, he's doing a good job, but we're a long way from proving any link to Mark. In fact—"

I was irked by Charles' lack of enthusiasm and angrily interrupted him, "Oh come on Charles! 'In fact' what? I know there's nothing to directly link Mark to Tessa yet, but can't you just admit that we're making good progress? Sharples has the evidence that Tessa's spending far more than she earns and that's the first step in proving that Mark's involved. Even if we don't find a link, it's got to look suspicious to a jury that Tessa's suddenly got lots of money to spend. As you would say: it's got to undermine her credibility."

While I could feel my face flushing as I spoke, Charles' demeanour didn't change at all. He waited calmly until I had finished my little rant and then he summarised the actual position we were in, rather the one I had been describing.

He started off by reiterating that he agreed that Sharples was doing a thorough and professional job. That, sadly, was the point at which his assessment of the situation diverged from mine.

"It does appear that Tessa has got some extra money from somewhere, but that money could have come from anywhere. Maybe she has inherited it, or been gifted it. It's possible that she, or Chris, have won some money gambling. Maybe it's a loan from somebody to help them out over Christmas and while Chris isn't working. Let me make it clear that, as things stand, there is no way that a judge would allow us to use this as evidence against Tessa. There is no proof of any wrongdoing or even of anything particularly suspicious."

The one thing that Charles and I did agree upon was that it was possible that Mark had bribed Tessa to make allegations against me. He qualified this, however, by saying that "almost anything was possible," and that as things stood there was absolutely no proof of any contact between Mark and Tessa, never mind any payment. In conclusion he said that it was his job to deal in the facts as they were presented to him and that in the long run I would not thank him if he gave me false hope.

I apologised to Charles for having snapped at him and decided that there was no point in discussing Sharples' findings any more that day. I realised that my excitement over the progress made by him was driven not by logic, but my desire to believe that this was the first step in proving that Mark and Tessa were working together. I couldn't expect Charles to see the significance of what had been achieved because he didn't really know or understand what Mark was like. He didn't know that Mark would do *anything* to win, especially if it meant beating me. He didn't know how Mark had turned, over the years, into a tyrant who completely dominated his wife. Most importantly, Charles didn't know that Mark used his wealth to get exactly what he wanted at all times. I knew my optimism was based on gut instinct rather than fact, but I also knew what Mark was capable of and I was convinced he had paid Tessa.

Despite my optimism about Sharples finding the link between Tessa and Mark, as my next court date loomed I was often enveloped by the familiar feelings of fear, frustration and isolation. Every morning I would wake up with a feeling of dread and a terrible fear of what was going to happen to me. Sometimes the feeling didn't leave me all day, particularly when I had nothing to do. Part of my frustration stemmed from the fact that most of the time there was nothing I could do, but wait. I tried to divert myself with exercise and too often I drank too much, but these things only gave me temporary respite from what felt like a huge weight bearing down on me. To a large extent I suffered these feelings of fear and frustration alone. Charles, Fergus and Sharples were all empathetic in the way that they dealt with me, but these relationships were professional rather than personal.

Although Jilly was undoubtedly in a better state of mind than she had been before she started taking her medication, she was still very vulnerable. I didn't feel that she was mentally strong enough for me to share the worst of my fears with her. My children were too young, and my father too old, for me to burden them. I needed to be strong for them, rather than the other way around. My sense of isolation was, if anything, heightened whenever I went for a drink with Joe Donnelly.

Although he hated Mark as much as I did, I didn't tell him anything significant about how my defence was progressing. There was always a risk that when he was drunk, and he was drunk a lot, that he would tell somebody what I had said and that it would get back to Mark. I felt that I had absolutely no one to turn to.

As the date for the preliminary hearing drew closer, my sense of fear, frustration and isolation was replaced by feelings of pure terror. Charles had assured me over and over again that this would simply be a matter of the judge setting a timetable for the trial, but I wasn't able to suppress my irrational fears. I imagined that I would be charged with something else or remanded in custody or found guilty there and then. When the 15th of January 2010 arrived and I found myself sitting in the Oakton Crown Court with Charles and Fergus, I was completely unable to function normally. Thankfully, as I had been told, repeatedly, by both of them, I didn't have to say anything. After it was all over and we had left the court I realised that I'd worked myself up into such a state that I didn't have a clue what had actually been decided during the preliminary hearing. When I asked Charles and Fergus what had happened, they looked at me quizzically. I explained that I'd been so nervous that it had all been a blur. Their quizzical looks turned to looks of concern and I realised that they were probably thinking how on earth I was going to cope when I was actually required to speak and give evidence. I presumed that was what they were thinking, because it was certainly what I was thinking.

Charles patiently went over what the judge had said, regarding the timetable of events, as we sat in a café close to the court. The prosecution had been given thirty days to serve their case to the defence lawyer and the court. A further twenty-one days later, the defence needed to submit the Defence Statement to the prosecution and the court. The judge had also set a date for the plea and case management hearing. This was to be on 17th February. Charles explained, not for the first time, that it was at the PCMH that I would enter my plea: not guilty. He also reminded me that if I pleaded guilty, I would get a twenty-five percent reduction in my sentence. This comment irritated me even though I knew he was just doing his job. The other crucial date that would be set at the PCMH was the trial date. Charles said that, technically, this should be about two months later, but because of general pressure on court time it could take significantly longer.

—

I met with Sharples once more before the PCMH. He had collected a huge amount of extra information about Tessa and he had extended his surveillance to include members of her family and some close friends. Some of the information he'd gathered, while not of any value to my cause was, nevertheless, of interest for other reasons. Sharples had discovered that Tessa and Chris spent a lot of time with their near neighbours Jean and Tony. They had kids of similar ages and the two couples socialised together every weekend. Tony was a big man with a big personality who, according to Sharples, dominated a room and certainly dominated his rather mousey wife, Jean. Jean was, seemingly, happy to be in her husband's shadow and lived an unremarkable life in all respects, except for one. Jean was sleeping with the nineteen-year-old son of her next-door neighbour. This didn't just happen occasionally, it happened every weekday. Ten minutes after Tony had gone to work and their children left for school, the boy next door would 'pop' next door and have sex with Jean. Sometimes he would 'pop' round in the afternoon as well. Sharples used the word 'pop' because, in order to indicate that the appropriate moment had arrived, Jean would send a text to the boy saying 'Pop round pet.' She also had photographs on her phone of the two of them 'in the act.' How Sharples got hold of these texts and photos I don't know, but, as was now always the case, neither Charles nor I asked.

Sharples relayed this information to us at the end of the meeting, after Charles had asked him whether there was anything else of note or interest that we should know about. Sharples had explained that there was something we might like to know, although he was careful to stress that it had nothing to do with the objective of the task. Unfortunately, the main part of his report was not as revelatory. There was nothing that materially improved my position. Tessa and Chris continued to spend more money than her wages would justify, but there was no indication of where this extra money was coming from. I forced myself to feel positive about this because, in my mind, the longer they continued to overspend, the more likely it was that the extra money was coming from Mark. I didn't bother to mention this to Charles as I knew what his response would be and I wanted to have something to hang on to.

—

Nothing much happened between my meeting with Sharples and the plea and case management hearing on 17th February. I was less nervous before this visit to court than I had been before some of my other appearances, and afterwards I did not need to ask Charles what had happened in the courtroom. I pleaded 'not guilty' and the trial was set for 14th June. This was nearly four months away and a full eight months since my arrest. The thought of being half way through the process was both unbearable and pleasing. On the one hand, I couldn't imagine how I could possibly endure another four months like the last four, and on the other, at least I knew when it would all be over. I hung on to the belief that four months would be long enough for Sharples to come up with the information needed to prove Mark's involvement.

Before I entered my plea, I was reminded again, by both Charles and Fergus, of the reduction in sentence I would get if I pleaded guilty. They also reminded me of the fact that, as things stood, it was the word of two women of good character against my word. They made great play of the fact that they were not trying to get me to change my plea, but it seemed a bit defeatist to me. As I left court, the cold reality hit me. This was going to happen. In four months time I would stand trial accused of raping two women. Depending on the outcome of the trial, I would either walk away as a free man with my reputation intact or I would go to prison for many years and my life would be ruined.

# Chapter 24

*Preparing for trial*

After the Christmas holiday, Max and Sam went back to school in high spirits. Jilly and I had done our best to make sure they'd been kept as busy as possible in order that they didn't become preoccupied with my situation. I also made sure that I presented a front that was confident and in control whenever we were in each other's company. When they asked me questions, I was as honest as I could be, while going into as little as detail as possible. It also helped that none of their friends, inside or outside school, seemed to be aware of my upcoming trial. Sadly, and I suppose inevitably, this changed within two weeks of their return to school. Max's best friend came into his bedroom late one evening and told him that he knew what was "happening with your father." The boy went on to tell Max that pretty much everybody in the school knew about it. When Max tried to laugh off what he had been told and asked his friend what exactly he was talking about, the response was very direct.

"Your dad has been accused of raping two women and he's going on trial later this year."

Max rang me up as soon as his friend had left the room and told me the news. It was something I had been expecting and had therefore planned for. I told Max to go and find Sam and explain the situation to him and then go directly to his housemaster's study. In the meantime, I phoned Mr Woodgate and told him what had happened and that I would be at the school within a couple of hours. When I arrived at the school, I found the boys in Mr Woodgate's study. Woodgate was his usual upbeat self, which contrasted with the glum and unsmiling look on the boys' faces.

Mr Woodgate and I tried to be as supportive as possible. He assured the boys that he would clamp down very hard on anyone who made comments about me and I encouraged them to focus on their schoolwork and sport. As it turned out, the other pupils made very few comments to them. What happened was worse than that and was very difficult for Max and Sam to cope with. They became increasingly isolated as the other boys, even their close friends, distanced themselves. No one said anything: they just stopped talking to them.

This continued into the Easter holidays. Their friends found reasons not to meet up with them. The boys were left with nothing to do but schoolwork. At least Max had his GCSEs to study for, Sam had no one to see and nothing to do. I tried my best to keep them entertained but it was a dreadful time for them. I had plenty to worry me, what with the trial approaching and the very real prospect of going to jail, but the thing I found most difficult to deal with was the impact on the boys. They were entirely innocent, but because of my actions with Rosie and the vindictive reaction of Mark, they were suffering terribly. My inability to do anything about this was almost overwhelming.

While their fellow pupils were distancing themselves from Max and Sam, Jilly was distancing herself from me. She was spending increasing amounts of time at work and had told me that she couldn't cope with discussing my case any more. She made it clear that unless there were dramatic developments either in my favour or against me, then she didn't want to know. I could feel her resentment towards me growing. I think the turning point in her attitude had come when I felt she was well enough for us to have a conversation about how much my defence was going to cost. When I explained that the cost might exceed a hundred thousand pounds, she became tearful and then furious. When she asked how on earth we were going to afford it, I had a ready response. I had investigated remortgaging our house and, even though it had lost over twenty percent of its value in the recession, I was confident that we would able to raise the money. I decided that any prospective lender did not need to know that my career, and therefore salary, could come to an abrupt end in a few months time.

Jilly argued about whether remortgaging was the right thing to do bearing in mind the recent fall in house prices. But when I asked for an alternative suggestion she did not have one. The discussion moved on to the boys school fees and how on earth she could afford them if the worst came to the worst and I was jailed. I had given this some thought and came to the conclusion that either the house or the school fees would have to go. When I said this to Jilly she reacted badly, but not in the way I had expected. I thought that there would be tears and then acceptance, instead there was vitriol and accusation. She spat the words out with a sneer on her face, "And all because you had to fuck Rosie."

"I'm sorry?"

"Whatever went on in that bedroom between you and Rosie, all this has happened because you just had to have her. You've always wanted her haven't you?"

"So, you don't believe me all of a sudden?"

"It doesn't matter whether I believe you or not, that's not for me to decide. What I'm saying is that if you hadn't screwed Rosie, none of this would have happened. You wouldn't be going to court and I wouldn't have to choose whether the boys lose their home or their chance of a good education."

Before I could respond to Jilly, she had stormed out of the house, slamming the front door as she went. Initially I was furious, but when I calmed down I was more a bit more philosophical about what she had said. Most of it was true. I *had* always wanted Rosie and it was true that if I hadn't had sex with her, then none of what followed would have happened. She was right that the boys' lives were going to be affected by what I had done, and the disruption to their lives was going to get much worse if I was found guilty. All of that was true, but it was the questioning of my innocence, which left a lasting impression on me. From then on, whenever I challenged her about it she always assured me that she believed in me completely, but I was never quite sure again.

—

What I needed was for Sharples to come up with something more than just evidence that Tessa was spending much more than she was earning. I needed him to find evidence that Mark was the source of the extra money. We had a meeting in early March at which he came up with the usual in-depth information about Tessa's cash purchases. This proved that he was working hard and earning his fees, but when I asked him what progress he'd made on the link with Mark, he just said, "None." He tried to continue talking about the new clothes, mobile phones and presents that Tessa had been buying for her family. This just irritated me. I wasn't interested in him justifying his existence. I wanted him to give me something that could be used in court. I told him to discontinue his "physical surveillance" and to concentrate solely on finding out where the money was coming from.

For the rest of March and for the next couple of months, my life spiralled downwards. Jilly's hostility towards me was growing as the trial approached. All sexual relations had ceased and, other than the two of us arguing about how was the best way to deal with the boys, we barely spoke. I lost my temper with her on a few occasions as she increasingly buried herself in her work and was in the house less and less. I accused her of giving up hope and not believing in me. She would challenge me to tell her what there was to be hopeful about and, when I couldn't come up with anything specific, she would storm off. If I cornered her about her lack of belief in me, she would offer an unconvincing and increasingly brief assurance that she didn't believe I had "broken the law." She left me with the impression, although she never said it, that she thought I had brought all of this upon myself. When she did talk at any length, it was to describe how terrible things were for her and the boys and how bleak things would become if I was found guilty. I couldn't argue with that.

Max and Sam continued to cope in very different ways. Sam ignored the fact that he was living an increasingly lonely existence at school. Mr Woodgate said he spent long hours alone in his room rather than being in the company of boys who were not speaking to him. Sam did not want to talk to either Jilly or me about the trial or to share his feelings with his brother. I noticed that when he was at home, he spent hour after hour with his nose in a book. Under normal circumstances I would have been pleased about this as he'd previously been reluctant to read at all, but these were not normal circumstances. Whenever I saw him reading it struck me as an attempt to escape from the real world and it made me terribly sad. Max, on the other hand, tried to create interaction with his friends at school by being confrontational and provocative. To some extent this was successful, as at least he got some response from the other boys even if it wasn't friendly. When he was at home he, at least, talked to me about his difficulties at school, but this didn't make me feel any less sad or guilty than did Sam's silence.

Every morning I woke up with the feeling that an enormous weight was bearing down on me. Most days I successfully managed to fight against this, almost unbearable, pressure. I would get up and get on with my life. Sometimes, however, I just couldn't face anything other than my bedroom and I would stay in bed all day hiding from the world. Jilly suggested that I go and see my doctor and tell him that I couldn't cope. She insisted that the doctor wouldn't judge me and that the pills she was taking had helped her feelings of anxiety and depression. I thought about taking her advice, but in the end I just couldn't do it. Something, deep inside me, told me that it was weak to give into these feelings. Maybe it was the way I had been brought up or some sort of old fashioned male pride but, whatever it was, I decided against getting medical help. That is not to say that I didn't use drugs to help me through my worst moments, it was just that the drugs I took were non-prescription and were drunk from a glass.

Mostly I drank alone, and when I did this, it would usually be vodka, but sometimes I would go for a beer with Joe Donnelly. I could always rely on him to be vicious about Mark and fully supportive of me. On a couple of occasions, after I had got particularly drunk, I let slip to Joe that I hadn't made much progress in terms of proving Mark had paid Tessa. He would encourage me to keep digging because not only was Mark "the sort of shit who would do anything to win," but he was also "an incredibly sneaky shit" who would cover his tracks. Even at the time, I think I realised that our conversations were the ramblings of a couple of bitter drunks, but they made me feel better for at least a few hours. Of course, the mornings after were some of my worst times. The naturally depressive after-effects of alcohol would make me feel more helpless and hopeless than ever.

As the trial date approached, the fear of what could happen began to exert an almost paralysing grip on me. When I thought of the worst scenario, one where I could spend anything up to ten years in jail, I would begin to shake uncontrollably. Sometimes I was physically sick. At other times, when I thought of how Mark had always managed to come out on top, I would be so consumed by resentment that I couldn't sleep for days on end. From the time I had first met him, he had always been 'number one.' He was better at sport, smarter and better liked. He had prettier girlfriends. He had lost his virginity first. He had gone to a better university and got a better degree. He had then landed a job I couldn't even have dreamed of. When, at last, I had won out, his reaction was to try to crush me and it was looking more and more likely that he would succeed.

I got some temporary relief from my feelings of guilt, fear, anger and terror whenever I met up with any members of my defence team. The meetings with Sharples were becoming less regular as he seemed to be making little, or no, progress. I retained his services more in hope than expectation. In contrast, the meetings with Fergus Pickard were becoming more frequent.

Fergus explained to me that when my case went to trial, his approach to each of the complainants would be very courteous. He said that if he treated both Rosie and Tessa gently and sympathetically in court then he would get more out of them. His basic tactic was to establish a rapport and get them to agree with his first few statements. After this, he claimed, they would be much more likely to agree with his next statement, even if they didn't want to. This would be done while all the time trying to keep them as calm as possible. Fergus was very keen on keeping them calm because, he explained, it was often the case that juries were distrustful of women who made claims of the worst type of sexual assault while remaining calm and collected throughout their evidence.

Fergus repeated what Charles had told me on many occasions. His intention was to completely undermine the credibility of Tessa and Rosie in the eyes of the jury. He did his best to explain how he would attempt to discredit them by maligning their behaviour both at the time of the alleged rapes and at other times. This would include focusing on the "foolishness" of their behaviour while he was cross-examining them. The jury would be invited to think that the defendant – me – could have reasonably believed that consent had been given. Fergus questioned me extensively about the clothes that the claimants were wearing when the alleged rapes happened. This was obviously not relevant as far as Rosie was concerned, but was seen as potentially significant in preparation for the cross examination of

Tessa. Related to all of this was the possibility of maligning the "sexual character" of the claimants. He emphasised that "sexual history" evidence was often relevant in cases where consent was the defence.

The problem was, that while I was completely satisfied that Fergus Pickard was the best man for the job, I was struggling to see how he was going to be able to mount a successful defence. Every time we met, I would leave with a positive attitude, but this would fade as the days passed. When I thought about how a jury might react to Tessa and Rosie, I was always left with the inescapable conclusion that they would react well to them. Tessa wasn't wearing provocative or sexy clothes on the night that we had sex and, to make things worse, we couldn't find anyone who was prepared to say that she *ever* dressed in a provocative way. Despite the chat amongst my school friends and I at the time, she was not, what would be considered, promiscuous. She had also been happily married for over fifteen years and there was no indication that she was immoral in any way. It seemed that Tessa was considered by everyone to be a pillar of the local community. It was apparent to me that the only thing in my favour was that she had come to the car with me willingly. I struggled to see how Fergus could effectively undermine her character or testimony in the eyes of the jury.

Rosie was, if anything, an even better prospective witness for the prosecution. There was no evidence to suggest that she ever dressed or acted in a sexually provocative way. I couldn't even find a photograph where she looked anything other than demure. She also appeared to have only ever had one lover, Mark. I had assumed that during the long periods before they were married and Mark was off 'sowing his wild oats,' that she had other relationships. Sadly, there was no evidence of this at all. She appeared to have been a 'one-man woman' and this was something that no doubt the prosecution would make a big deal of. Our main hope with Rosie was that the intimacy that she and I had enjoyed on that fateful Sunday would be something that could be used against her. Unfortunately, the staff at the Cottage had either not seen the intimate moments between us or had interpreted them differently from me. The most that any of the staff were prepared to say was that we had appeared to be "very comfortable" in each other's company. At one stage, I had even considered that Mark had perhaps got to them as well, but even for Mark that would have been too much of a risk.

In my own mind, my main hope of clearing my name remained proving that Tessa had been paid to make her allegation. Frustratingly, there was still no positive news from Sharples. Charles and Fergus had never really bought into the idea that Mark had paid Tessa. In the last six weeks before the trial, neither of them even mentioned the possibility of this being a part of the defence case that they were constructing. I continued to pay Sharples a reduced monthly fee because I couldn't think of what else to do. Meanwhile,

Charles and Fergus concentrated on ways in which they could undermine or malign the character and evidence of Tessa and Rosie. I couldn't see how this would be successful on its own, but of course I had never been involved in a trial before so I wasn't best placed to make a judgement. Fergus was always keen to stress that you could never tell what sort of a witness someone would be until they were actually in court, giving evidence.

As my confidence ebbed away, I looked to Charles to give me some comfort. Increasingly, it looked like I would be reliant upon Fergus pulling off an amazing feat of legal escapology for me to avoid prison. I wanted Charles to tell me that the odds were much better than that. As had always been the case, he was unwilling to offer me false hope. As the trial approached he confirmed my worst fears. He said that, all things being equal, I would probably be found guilty. Although he was merely confirming what I already strongly suspected, it still came as a hammer blow. I was in shock and, although I continued to ask him questions and I could hear his responses, it was as if I was outside my own body looking at someone else. A week before the trial, he told me that if there was no new evidence, and Tessa and Rosie proved to be good witnesses, then Fergus was going to have a very difficult task in discrediting them. He didn't say that there was no hope, but I knew there was a strong possibility that I would be going to jail.

# Chapter 25

## *The trial*

For most of the week running up to the trial I remained in, what can only be described as, a state of shock. I acted in, what must have seemed like, a normal way to anyone observing me, but I felt numb and detached. My state of detachment was interrupted only occasionally as feelings of terror and helplessness rushed in on me. I could not control when this happened, but whenever it did I would become breathless and have to sit down in order to avoid falling down. A couple of times I was convinced I was having a heart attack. These interruptions didn't last long and I was relieved when they were over and I returned to my dreamlike state. Neither Charles nor Fergus saw me in these states of near physical collapse and, at separate times, they both complimented me on my calmness. They believed that this would be an asset in court whereas I feared I would crumble under the strain of it all.

The last couple of days before the trial flashed by. My feelings of wishing time would pass more quickly, so that at least it would all be over, were replaced by wanting time to go more slowly. And then, all of a sudden, the waiting was over. On a sunny day in mid June 2010, I found myself in Oakton Crown Court on trial for the rape of two women. There had been no last minute withdrawal of allegations and no significant new evidence. It was actually happening.

I arrived at Oakton Crown Court at 9 a.m. and Charles, Fergus and I had our final meeting before the proceedings started. The meeting was just to establish that there had been no last minute developments. There were none. At 9.45 a.m. I found myself sitting next to the custody officer, in the dock, towards the back of the court. At the front of the court was an empty bench on a raised platform where the judge would shortly be seated. The rest of the court was full of people, but the only ones I was concerned with were the members of the jury. They were standing in small groups on the left hand side of the court. This surprised me as I assumed that they would be seated in the jury box.

The jury box was situated along the sidewall to the right of me and remained empty. I presumed that the jury would take their seats before the arrival of the judge at 10 a.m., but this didn't happen. I didn't look directly at the small groups of jurors but I could feel their eyes burning into me. This was, of course, the first time we had been in each other's presence and they were no doubt as fascinated by me as I was by them. The advantage they had over me was that they could look directly at me to get their first impressions. I could only glance at them while making sure that I did not make direct eye contact with anybody.

Despite the fact that my whole body was shaking uncontrollably, I tried to use my body language to give the jury the best possible first impression. This wasn't something that Fergus had specifically briefed me on, but it seemed very important at the time. I tried to convey to the jury that I was open, honest, non-threatening and most of all, innocent of any crime. I very much doubt that I managed to convey anything other than sheer terror. Thankfully, Charles, who was seated directly in front of me, turned around a couple of times to give me encouraging looks. This gave me something to do other than *not* look at the jury. He didn't actually say or signal anything either of the times that he looked around, but it gave me the opportunity to nod my head at him on the first occasion and look behind me at the public gallery on the second. These simple actions gave me the opportunity to peripherally glance at the jury. I didn't learn anything by doing this, other than that they seemed to be fairly evenly split between men and women and were of a variety of different ages.

At 10 a.m. the judge entered from a side door next to the raised platform at the front of the court. Just as he did this, the clerk of the court rose to his feet and shouted, "All Rise."

I, along with everybody else, got to my feet and stared out over the court. I couldn't believe that this was actually happening to me. When the judge was seated, everybody took their seats except for the jurors who remained standing in their little groups. They were all staring at the judge, so I took the chance to have a proper look at them for the first time. Two things struck me. They were a nondescript group of people and there were more than twelve of them. I suddenly remembered that Charles had told me that before the trial got underway the jury would be empanelled.

This process took a couple of hours and by the time the final twelve jurors were selected, and had taken their seats in the jury box, it was after 12 noon. The judge then announced to, what seemed to me to be, a court full of smiling faces that he was a "bit peckish" and that we would adjourn for lunch. For the first time in a long while, I emerged from my 'dream state' to feel irritation rather than just fear. I was careful not to show anyone in the court how I felt, but I couldn't believe how relaxed everyone seemed. There I was, facing prison and ruination, while the judge and jury smiled at each other and discussed lunch.

—

The desperate situation in which I found myself, hit me with renewed force on the first afternoon of the trial. The prosecution barrister gave his opening address to the court. He began by telling the jury why we were all there. He was economical with his words when he told them that there had been two allegations of rape made against the defendant. The jurors turned their heads from the prosecuting barrister to me and then back to the barrister. He outlined what I was accused of, how he was going to prove his case and the witnesses he was going to call.

At some point during the prosecution barrister's opening statement, my attention was drawn to the public gallery behind me. Somebody was having a coughing fit. The barrister paused until the coughing stopped and I looked around instinctively to see what was going on. For some reason, I hadn't even thought about who would be in the public gallery other than my own family. Jilly was intending to take time off work to show her support, but did not attend on that first day. My father was there, as he would be every day of the trial. To my horror, the first faces I saw when I turned around were very familiar to me. In the front row of the gallery sat Mark, Patrick and Patrick's wife, Katie. The look on Mark's face managed to convey contempt, superiority and confidence as he stared, unflinchingly, at me.

I found Mark's presence in the court extremely unsettling. While I should have been listening to every word the barrister was saying, I found myself contemplating the part that Mark had played in putting me in the dock and how determined he would be to see me punished for what I had done with Rosie. I thought about all the times he had won out against me and I had a terrible, sinking feeling that it was going to happen yet again.

The sinking feeling didn't leave me the next day. The accusation made by Rosie was dealt with first. Detective Sergeant Lane entered the witness box to give evidence relating to the interview that she had given when she first made her allegation to the police. He read out the questions that had been asked during the interview and the prosecution barrister read out the answers given by Rosie. All the time that this was going on, I could feel the jurors' eyes boring into me. The evidence from the interview was stark and damning and, to my ears, full of lies and omissions. There was no mention of Rosie crying because of the state of her marriage or of me comforting her. There was no mention of the intimate day that the two of us had spent together. The description of how I had entered her bedroom and, without saying anything, had raped her was sickening.

Later on that day, Rosie was called to the witness box to be questioned by the prosecution. As she approached the box, I could see that she had lost weight since I last saw her in October. Even then she had been on the verge of being underweight, but now she looked very frail. Rosie was dressed in a dark blue business suit and her hair was pulled back off her face. She wore very little, if any, makeup. I looked over my right shoulder to where I knew Jilly, who was at court on that second day, would be in the public gallery. She was seated next to my father and was dabbing at her eyes with a handkerchief. It was a horrible situation for everybody, but I didn't have the capacity to think beyond how Rosie's appearance would play on the sympathy of the jury. She looked tiny and very vulnerable.

The prosecution barrister began by setting the scene for the court. He asked Rosie about the relationship between her, Jilly, Mark and I. He asked her about the closeness and trust that existed between four friends who had known each other for nearly thirty years. Rosie gave her answers in a very small voice and, on a couple of occasions, the judge had to ask her to speak up so that the court could hear her properly. When her barrister asked questions about her relationship with Mark, her voice started to break and the judge offered her a glass of water and gently instructed her to stay calm and take her time. I thought in my naivety that she might describe a long-term relationship, which had been under strain in recent times. Instead she described Mark as her one and only love, a man that she adored – the only man she had ever been with.

Whenever Rosie became too emotional to continue, I studied the reaction of the jury. Some of them looked genuinely concerned for her and I could only imagine that they were thinking – why would such a woman make up these allegations? What they didn't know was how Mark completely dominated and controlled her and how she would do, or say, anything for him.

When the barrister's questions turned to the specifics of what had happened on that Sunday in October, Rosie became ever more overwrought. As she described the activities of the day that she and I had shared, she broke down completely. There were lengthy breaks as she tried to re-compose herself. In between her sobs and breaks for water, Rosie described a long-term friendship, which had never been anything but platonic and was based on trust. The way she described it, the time we had spent together during the day on Sunday was relaxing and innocent. There was no hint of the type of intimacy that could have led me, or anyone else, to believe that it was anything other than an enjoyable day on which two old friends were thrown together through circumstance.

By the time the questioning turned to what had happened after dinner on that fateful evening, Rosie was in a terrible state. Her eyes were red and puffy, and her voice was so shaky that the judge had to ask her to speak up once more. She managed to describe our dinner together and the two of us going outside for a cigarette after the meal was finished. She also told the court that she had very little to drink throughout the evening. She described me as drinking heavily during the meal. It was obvious to me that the frail and very distressed figure in the witness box was extracting enormous sympathy from everyone in the court. I tried to make myself look as distressed as Rosie but, even as I was attempting to do this, I was aware that, in the jury's eyes, the contrast between the two of us could not have been greater.

When her barrister asked Rosie how she had reacted to me entering her bedroom, her sobs became even louder. It was just possible to hear her say that she was half asleep when she heard the door to her room open. She claimed that she was terrified when she first became aware that there was someone in her room, and that it took her some time before her eyes adjusted to the darkness and she realised that it was me. Rosie was able to compose herself as she described how her initial relief at realising that it was me in her room, turned quickly to fear. She told the court that I walked across the bedroom and sat down on the edge of her bed and silently stared at her. At this point Rosie began sobbing again. After another glass of water, she was asked to continue. With her head bowed, she told the court that she sat up and asked me what I was doing in her bedroom. She then said that, without saying a word, I forced her head back on to the pillow and started to climb on top of her. As she spoke there was a deathly hush in the court. Her barrister waited a few moments before asking her "What happened next?"

Rosie swallowed hard before telling the court that she said, "Please stop Tom."

She then told the court that I had put my hand over her mouth and raped her.

—

After lunch, Rosie was cross-examined by Fergus. He began his cross-examination by confirming the details of the day we had spent together. He spoke in a quiet and reassuring voice as he asked Rosie whether she had enjoyed the various aspects of the day. Without ever using the exact words, he managed to suggest to Rosie that we had shared an intimate time together. He asked his questions in a way that left Rosie no alternative but to agree that she had spent an idyllic day with me and that she had been a "willing participant" in that day. When Fergus turned his attention to the point at which I entered her room, he continued to speak in a very quiet and calm voice.

Rosie began to get upset almost as soon as Fergus started cross-examining her on exactly what had happened in the bedroom. He suggested that, rather than offer any resistance to me, she had, through her actions, consented wholeheartedly. He used the phrase "willing participant" repeatedly and every time he did, Rosie became more upset. When she was challenged directly about the nature of our "lovemaking", she began to hyperventilate. She gasped for air in exactly the same way as she had done on that Sunday afternoon when she described to me the state of her marriage to Mark. The judge tried to calm her down so that she could continue to give her evidence, but it became apparent pretty quickly that she was not going to be able to continue. Eventually the judge ordered an adjournment and Rosie was led away from the witness box by one of the members of the prosecution team.

The judge gave Rosie as much time as he could to recover her composure, but eventually it was decided that she couldn't continue. She did not return to the witness box and the judge adjourned the court for the rest of the day. I found out much later, she actually spent that night in hospital, heavily sedated. Under virtually all other circumstances, I would have been concerned for my old friend but, understandably, I felt no sympathy for her at all. As far as I was concerned she had allowed herself to be bullied by Mark into making false claims against me and she was now suffering the consequences of her own weakness.

Immediately after the proceedings were adjourned for the day, a meeting was held in the judge's chambers with both the defence and prosecution barristers. Charles explained to me that because Rosie was unable to continue, Fergus was going to put it to the judge that she couldn't complete the process of giving evidence and therefore that there was no case to answer. For the first time in days, my spirits lifted.

"Does this mean that the whole case against me will collapse?" I asked Charles as we waited outside the judge's chambers.

Charles, as usual, was measured in his response, "I don't think it's wise for me to predict what is going to be decided in chambers. It's best we wait and see what Fergus has to say."

I wasn't going to let Charles dampen my high hopes as easily as that.

"What is the best case scenario? Is there any chance that Rosie's evidence will be dismissed?"

Charles looked at me and paused for a while before saying, "There's a chance that the judge will decide that, because Rosie hasn't been able to complete the cross-examination, her evidence does not 'come up to proof.'"

I didn't know exactly what he meant by "come up to proof", but I decided not to push him any further. I wanted to believe that things were finally turning in my favour. I was desperate to hang on to the hope that maybe things could still turn out all right.

When Fergus joined Charles and I in the little side room that had been allocated to us, I couldn't tell from the expression on his face whether it was good news or bad. It turned out to be mostly bad news. The judge had decided that although Rosie's inability to continue under cross-examination made her a poor witness, that there was still a case to answer. My first reaction was to blame Fergus for not being able to convince the judge. I temporarily lost control and had a bit of a foul-mouthed rant at him. He stayed very calm and waited for me to finish my outburst. He explained that he'd pushed the judge very hard on whether the case should continue, bearing in mind that one of the alleged victims couldn't give proper evidence. The judge had, however, been adamant that because of the evidence Rosie had given before the trial to the police, and during the trial when questioned by the prosecution barrister, that the trial would continue. Apparently, he had stressed to Fergus that if Rosie had been the only complainant then maybe things would be different but, with Tessa still to give her evidence, he felt it was right to continue.

That night, alone in my hotel bedroom, I felt as low as I had ever done. I went over and over in my mind the events of the day and each time I did, I was more convinced that I was going to be found guilty. Fergus had reassured me that he would do everything he could to make sure that he undermined Rosie's evidence, or lack of it, in the eyes of the jury. He believed that he had a chance of convincing them that her inability to answer questions under cross-examination was grounds for a reasonable doubt. I didn't share his confidence. The jury had, in my opinion, reacted very positively to Rosie. I had seen the looks of sympathy in their eyes as this obviously distressed woman of impeccable character gave her evidence. I came to the conclusion that, if I were in their shoes, I couldn't have seen any reason for her to lie. My night wasn't just sleepless, it was panic stricken. A couple of times I was on the verge of calling Charles or Jilly because I felt so unwell. The terrifying thought of being found guilty and going to prison didn't just scare me it made me feel as if I would have some sort of seizure.

—

I arrived at court the next day feeling exhausted. Charles did his best to raise my spirits by pointing out that Tessa was due to start giving evidence that morning and that he doubted she would be able to evoke as much sympathy from the jury as Rosie obviously had. I felt too tired to do anything other than smile weakly at him. If I'd had the energy, I would have asked him to go over, once more, how Fergus was planning to handle Tessa's cross-examination, but I left it at a weak smile.

The prosecution barrister questioned Tessa for most of the day. Her evidence perfectly matched everything she had told the police when she made her allegations against me. Unlike Rosie, she seemed to be in control of her emotions. A couple of times her voice wavered as she was asked particularly intrusive questions, but for the most part, she was calm and precise. The longer her evidence went on, the worse I felt. I couldn't help but think that the jury would feel the same way towards her as, in my mind, they felt about Rosie. Why would such a respectable woman – a devoted wife and mother – make this up? They knew nothing of Mark or the lengths that he would go to get revenge on me, and Fergus had ruled out even introducing the concept to the jury of Mark having bribed Tessa. He'd explained that, after a promising start, Sharples had not produced any usable evidence of anything illegal having happened.

By the time the prosecution barrister had finished questioning Tessa, it was after 3 p.m. The judge decided that it was too late for Fergus to begin his cross-examination and proceedings were adjourned for the day. Fergus and Charles decided that no real purpose would be served by having another meeting until the following morning, so we went our separate ways. I suspected that they were using the early finish to get back home to London and that suited me. I had not been home for a couple of days, so I decided that I would make the journey back to London as well. When I got home I found the house empty. I had phoned Jilly before I left Wiltshire to let her know I was on my way back and I was disappointed that she wasn't at home when I arrived. After coming to court on the second day of the trial, she had decided not to attend again until things were coming to a conclusion. I saw her absence as a lack of support, but I knew better than to challenge her. It would only end up in an argument and I couldn't face that.

When Jilly arrived home from work, I was already half way through a bottle of red wine. She joined me in the sitting room and helped me to finish the bottle. She listened to my description of the day's activities and, while she made supportive comments, she seemed distant. It was as if she was doing her duty by saying the right things, while at the same time preparing for me to be found guilty. When she suggested that she go into the kitchen to prepare supper, I got the feeling that she didn't want to be in the same room as me. We ate supper in relative silence and, when we'd finished, she asked me if I minded if she went to bed as she was very tired.

I slept in the spare room that night so that I didn't disturb her. I didn't have the energy to properly consider her behaviour. I felt that I was losing her, just like I had lost my friends, my colleagues and my reputation. The only people who still seemed to be on my side were my father and my sons. I slept fitfully. It seemed like every time I dropped off to sleep, I would wake up with a start and in a cold sweat. When my alarm went off at 5 a.m. the next morning, I was already awake. I felt completely drained, but I was glad to get up so that I didn't have to try and sleep anymore. I needed to be at the court by 8.30 a.m. for my scheduled meeting with Fergus and Charles, so I showered and shaved quickly and was on my way by 5.30 a.m.

Unsurprisingly, there was very little traffic on the road at that time in the morning and I arrived outside the court at just after 7.30 a.m. Suddenly, my tiredness caught up with me and so I parked a couple of streets away and dozed off. I woke with a start, not knowing how long I had been asleep, and worried that I might be late for my meeting with Fergus and Charles. When I looked at the clock in the car I realised I had only been asleep for half an hour or so. My anxiety about being late was immediately replaced by a terrible nervousness about what the day ahead held in store. I knew that if Tessa performed well under cross-examination from Fergus, that things were going to look very bleak for me.

When I arrived at the court, I made my way to the little meeting room that had been allocated to my defence team. I was twenty minutes early, but I was confident that Charles would already be there as he was always early for our meetings. We would be able to have a chat before Fergus turned up. I was hopeful, that just by talking to him, the terrible feeling of dread which had descended upon me, might somehow be alleviated. To my surprise neither of them were in the meeting room. I decided to go and get myself a coffee while I waited for them. When I returned to the meeting room there was still no sign of them. I'd found a copy of yesterday's newspaper beside the coffee machine so I settled down to read it while I waited. Much as I tried to interest myself in the various news stories, I couldn't. Even when I read the sports pages I found that nothing registered.

Half an hour later, there was still no sign of Charles or Fergus. I was getting a little annoyed at their lateness and finally decided to check my mobile to see if either of them had left a message. It was only then that I realised that I hadn't switched it on. I'd turned it off the previous night, and completely forgotten to turn it on again. I had two missed calls, both from Charles. My immediate fear was that either he or Fergus were ill and wouldn't be attending court. Charles had left two voicemails, one at 7 a.m. and the other at 8 a.m. The first message was a request for me to call him urgently, and the second was to let me know that he would not be at our meeting until after 9 a.m. because he had an unscheduled meeting with the prosecution team. This just confirmed my fears that Fergus was probably ill and that he wouldn't be able to carry out the cross-examination of Tessa that day. I called Charles but his mobile went straight to voicemail.

The hour of nine came and went and there was still no sign of Charles. I stared at the newspaper and tried to interest myself in something – anything – that I was reading, but again nothing registered. Finally, the door opened and in walked Charles followed by Fergus. I'd convinced myself that Fergus was ill, so his presence surprised me. I got to my feet but, before I could utter a word, Charles put up his hand to silence me. He was smiling broadly.

"Get ready to smile," he said.

"What is it?" I replied

I noticed that Fergus was also smiling. This confused me, as he had always been very serious in all the meetings I'd had with him. Before I could try to work out what was going on, Charles was speaking again.

"I got a call from our man Sharples late last night saying that he'd got the evidence he needed to prove that Mark paid Tessa to make her allegation of rape."

I stared at him and tried to work out what he was saying. I had agreed to keep Sharples on his reduced retainer right up until the trial, but had given up any realistic hope of him finding anything. I hadn't actually thought about him, or his investigation, since the beginning of the trial. I remained silent while Charles continued.

"The documents that he has got his hands on, prove that on November 11th last year Mark made a payment of thirty-five thousand pounds into an account that Tessa has indirect access to. We have presented these documents to the prosecution and, after speaking to Tessa, they have accepted that Mark has made this payment. The prosecution have agreed that, before the jury are called into the court, they will inform the judge that their witness has been paid and that they can offer no further evidence in this case."

Initially, I couldn't take in what Charles was saying. While he and Fergus stood there smiling, I just stared blankly at them. Eventually I managed to gather my jumbled thoughts.

"What... what proof has Sharples come up with?" I asked.

Charles didn't answer my question. He was now not only smiling, he was pumping his fists in the air, as if he had just scored the winning goal in a cup final. Fergus, who was also still smiling from ear to ear, then moved towards me grabbed my hand and started to shake it vigorously. At this stage I was unable to process what Charles had told me. I don't know whether it was shock, but I just couldn't let myself believe what I was hearing. I finally managed to gather myself and asked again, this time in a slightly raised and agitated voice

"What proof has Sharples come up with?"

Charles stopped pumping his fists and started to explain, "It's quite complicated, but Sharples has proof that Mark transferred thirty-five thousand pounds, via two companies that he controls, to a friend of Tessa's mother. This friend has then withdrawn some of the money, in cash, from this account and given it to Tessa. Sharples has photographs of the woman, in Tessa's house, giving her some of the cash. He also has proof that the account was set up by a company in Switzerland and that Mark has control of this company via another company registered in The Isle of Man."

Charles then moved towards me, put his arms around me and gave me a huge bear hug. Although I had understood what Charles had told me, I was still unwilling to join in with his celebrations. I had far too many questions that I wanted to ask him.

"How has Sharples got this information?"

Charles stepped back from me and, with the smile still fixed on his face, wagged his finger and gently admonished me.

"Now now, Tom. You know better than to ask me that. All you need to know is that Sharples' evidence has been accepted by the prosecution and that they will be telling the judge that they can offer no further evidence because their witness has been paid."

"What does this mean?"

"It means Tom, that once he has been told by the prosecution that they can offer no evidence, the judge will call the jury into the court and tell them that this case will no longer proceed."

"Are you *absolutely* sure?"

"Yes, Tom. I am absolutely positive."

"Is it possible that the judge could decide that the case can continue anyway?"

"No, Tom. Believe me when I tell you that it is

definitely over. There is no chance that the trial will continue."

I didn't finally allow myself to believe Charles until I was in front of the judge and he told me that I was free to go. At that point I did allow myself to smile, but I felt no sense of triumph as I left the court, just overwhelming relief. My nightmare was suddenly, and completely unexpectedly, over.

When I got outside the court, the first person that I saw was my father. I rushed towards him and we wrapped our arms around each other. Suddenly, I felt weak and incredibly shaky on my feet. I extracted myself from my father's embrace and went to sit on a low wall nearby. I sat with my hands on my knees with my head bowed and took some deep breaths. My father followed me to the wall, took my head in his hands and held it to his chest. I was taking huge gulps of air. As my father stroked my hair he quietly said, "Let it out son. You've been strong enough for long enough. Now just let it out."

And with his permission, I allowed myself to cry for the first time since I was a child.

# Diary Extract

## *June 2014*

I can't believe I've finally finished writing my 'story'. It's taken me two years. I don't suppose anybody will ever read it, but it's not really intended for public consumption. It just felt like something I needed to do. I will probably just hide it away with the rest of my diaries. My account of the events of the period from the Autumn 2009 to the collapse of my trial in June 2010 is based on the diary that I wrote during that period. I will be eternally grateful to Charles for insisting that I kept this record. Every entry was made from the perspective of an innocent man. I read and re-read all my entries again and again to make sure that I remained consistent in my description of the events. I told the same story whether I was talking to Jilly, the police, Charles, Fergus, or anybody else.

But it wasn't just the fact that I kept a diary that enabled me to convince those close to me that I was innocent. My behaviour, when I was initially arrested and taken to Wiltshire for questioning, was also vital. I am proud of how I conducted myself when first confronted on my doorstep by the police. I could easily have said the wrong thing to Detective Sergeant Lane when he arrested me. Equally, I could also have said the wrong thing once I was taken to Overbury Police Station. It's difficult to explain just how traumatic those first few hours at the police station were. Yes, I'd had some time on the journey to Wiltshire to plan how I would play it, but it could have gone very wrong. I could have tried to get by without the help of Charles and said something really stupid. I didn't, and I'm still impressed with how I reacted under huge strain. I'm sure Mark thought that I would crack under the pressure almost immediately.

Since those dark and desperate days of 2009 and 2010, life has improved immeasurably for me. In those dismal times, I never expected to be able to feel this way ever again, but I am happy. When you are charged with the most horrific crimes, whether you are innocent or not, an all-pervading air of suspicion surrounds you. People don't openly accuse you, but they will ignore you completely or react in a way that indicates that they don't trust you. Mostly they keep their distance. This extends to your family. I still feel guilty for the pain, fear and isolation that my two boys suffered at school. The school authorities made sure that they weren't openly victimized, but they lost friends and were not invited anywhere, or included by anyone in any activity, for a long time. The accusations levelled at me translated into a guilty verdict for Jilly and the boys until the moment the trial collapsed.

My feelings of happiness and contentment have, ironically, been at least partially enabled by Mark. If I had been arrested but not charged because of lack of evidence, or even if I had been found not guilty by a jury, I am sure that, in some quarters, the finger of suspicion would still be pointed at me. The actions of Mark, which led to the case completely collapsing, have ensured that, in the eyes of the world, I have, not just been found to be innocent of any crime, but that my innocence is proven beyond any doubt. The world believes that he bullied Rosie into making a false accusation and that he bribed Tessa to outright lie. He nearly won, but in the end his loss was catastrophic.

Mark doesn't even live in the UK now. Less than a year after my trial collapsed, his began. It was obvious to everyone, after the payments to Tessa were uncovered, that, not only would I go free, but that Mark would face charges. He was charged and found guilty of perverting the course of justice. The specific charge was 'conspiring with another to pervert the course of justice'. Mark hired the most expensive defence team that money could buy, but it did him no good. He was sentenced to three years in prison and served nearly two years of that sentence. He was released a couple of years ago and, the last I heard of him, he was living in Argentina. He's still got his millions but, the reports I get from the few people that have been in touch with him indicate that, he's a broken and bitter man.

Tessa was also charged with perverting the course of justice and was given a similar sentence to Mark. I haven't heard anything about her since she was released. Tessa claimed at her trial that, although she was paid by Mark to give evidence against me, her testimony was true. Was her testimony true? I don't think so. In 1980 things were really quite different from the way they are now. Girls at that time often said "no" when they actually meant, "yes." They said "no" so that they wouldn't have to take responsibility for their sexual urges and, perhaps, so that in their own minds they weren't 'easy.' When she said "Please stop, Tom," to me, I just thought she was playing hard to get. I still think that.

Rather incredibly, I'm rich and successful now. When Jilly and I went away for that weekend in the autumn of 2009 with Mark and Rosie, things were very different. I definitely didn't have a successful career. In fact, I was very worried that I'd lose my job. We had, what seemed like, a huge mortgage on a home that had just lost twenty per cent of its value, I was stuck in a dead end job and had years of school fees to pay. We then had to remortgage our home in London to fund my defence. How have I become rich? Well, quite frankly it's not really down to anything clever that I've done. I've become rich because my house is now worth a fortune. Jilly and I stretched ourselves to the limit when we bought our three bedroom terraced house in 1996. We paid two hundred and forty nine thousand for a shabby little house with a smallish garden. Yes, Parsons Green was a nice area even then, and yes, we have added another bedroom and extended the kitchen, but we had no idea just how 'clever' we had been. It's now worth just under two million pounds. What seemed like a huge mortgage in 2010 is now a relatively small and inexpensive one. We did absolutely nothing 'clever' and have become rich. It's pure luck, but I suppose after what I've been through I deserve a bit of luck.

How have I become successful? Well, that's got precious little to do with me either. After I was arrested, I was suspended from work on full pay. I remained on full pay until the trial was over and then for another three months until I was required to return to work. I even got a pay rise while I was suspended. When I returned to work, I was treated with kid gloves. No one ever made any mention of what had happened and everybody went out of his or her way to treat me fairly. A year after I returned to work, I was encouraged by my boss to apply for a job that was being both internally and externally advertised. It was a position that I felt unqualified to do either by experience or talent. Before I was arrested, it was a job for which I wouldn't even have bothered to apply. There was a three-stage interview process but it was obvious to me, after twenty minutes of the first interview, that I was going to get it. My theory is that someone at a senior level decided that, in order to avoid being accused of discriminating against me, it was best that they positively discriminated in my favour. The company has had to employ someone else to help me do the job, but no one would ever dare to say so. It might be seen as discriminating against me and everyone is paranoid about being seen to do that. I now earn more than double what I earned in 2009. I even earn more than Jilly.

Jilly's attitude to me now is much changed. She respects the progress I have made in my business career over the last few years. I like being respected in this way and I have no intention of sharing my theories as to why, after years of floundering at work, I have in the last few years become a 'dynamic over-achiever'. I think I'll keep that one to myself. All I know is that, rather than being dismissive of my opinions on the corporate world and business in general, Jilly is now rapt with attention every time I pronounce on new methodologies or developments in business strategy. She is also much more respectful to me in terms of her dealings with other men. We have been to quite a few work and social events in the last few years and whereas she used to spend the whole time flirting outrageously, she is now relentlessly attentive to me. The boot is now firmly on the other foot and Jilly makes sure that she appears at my shoulder whenever I'm talking to any attractive women. Maybe Mark was right all along. He always made it quite clear to me that Jilly's affair was somehow my fault and that if I hadn't been so devoted and faithful to her, then she wouldn't have taken me for granted and strayed. Is that really the way it works? I think perhaps it is.

Whether it's my more senior position at work or my change in attitude, I don't know, but I am apparently much more desirable to the opposite sex than I have ever been before. This makes me more confident which, in turn, seems to make me even more attractive. For me, it is a 'virtuous circle'. Jilly has noticed this and has, on occasion, got quite annoyed with me when she considers my flirting has got out of hand. It's almost a complete role reversal, and one that I am quite enjoying. I know I shouldn't have, but on a few occasions I have taken advantage of my new found power over women. I sort of justify this to myself in a number of ways. Firstly, if Jilly hadn't started this cycle of deception then I don't think I would have. If I hadn't felt so undermined, so emasculated, so powerless, then I don't think that what happened with Rosie would have taken place. I needed to re-establish my confidence and self respect somehow. Secondly, the fact that my life has improved on almost all levels has definitely made me more of a 'carpe diem' sort of man. I took my chance with Rosie, I seized the day, and although it almost ended in disaster, it didn't. I now believe that taking a risk, being a bit reckless, will pay off. I am as successful, confident and content a man as I have ever been.

The same cannot be said of Rosie. She is in a terrible way. Although she didn't actually complete her evidence against me in court, she is held at least partially responsible by most of our extended group of friends for the ordeal that Jilly, the boys and I went through. I think the consensus is that being weak and malleable is not really an excuse. Most people think that if she had never allowed herself to be manipulated by Mark's desire for revenge, then we wouldn't have gone through the tortuous time that we did. She didn't face any charges after the trial collapsed, but she was found unofficially guilty by almost everybody of appalling and unforgivable behaviour.

I say found guilty by 'almost' everybody, because there are a few of our mutual friends who have maintained a relationship with Rosie and did, at least for a while, express concern for her plight. Jilly would become extremely angry and agitated whenever anybody even hinted at sympathy for Rosie. This, on a couple of occasions, ended up in public and pretty vitriolic verbal attacks by Jilly on whomever dared to exhibit anything other than total contempt for Rosie. Rather unsurprisingly, this resulted in an almost complete silence on the matter. The one person who remained a public supporter of Rosie, for an extended period, was her brother Patrick. He was completely supportive of both Mark and Rosie during the trial and continued to support them even after it was decided I had no case to answer. Joe Donnelly told me that, not only had Patrick continued to publicly support Rosie's claims, but those made by Tessa as well. I decided not to get angry about this, but to get Charles Burton involved again. Charles sent Patrick a letter warning him about repeating his views in public. Since that letter was sent, nothing has been heard from Patrick on the subject.

Rosie doesn't go out much now. This is partly because Mark left her and the children poverty stricken when he went to Argentina, and partly because she has been, to a large extent, socially ostracised. She really has thrown it all away because of the ridiculous way in which she has behaved. She has made the wrong choices almost all of her adult life. Without wishing to be arrogant, her first bad choice was not picking me when I made it so obvious I liked her when she came to visit me at university. If she had given me any encouragement, I would have picked her over Jilly and she must have known that. We got on very well, we made each other laugh and we were well-suited.

I suppose you can't force yourself to fancy someone just because you are well-suited, but she surely should have seen that I was a better bet than Mark. Yes, Mark had a lot going for him, but it must have been obvious that he wouldn't make her happy in the long run. Even when he was a student there were lots of women surrounding Mark and he was casual with their feelings to the point of cruelty. I think we all knew that he would be successful, but there was never any chance he would be faithful. Rosie continued to choose Mark over me – and everyone else – even after he repeatedly proved himself to be unreliable. On the many occasions that they broke up when they were young, and he had relationships with other people, Rosie was always more than willing to have him back when he decided that it was a good idea. She should have known that if you keep making bad decisions then eventually there will be bad consequences.

That's certainly what happened when she decided to tell Mark what had happened that night at the Cottage, and then again when she allowed herself to be bullied into going to the police about it. What a stupid bitch. We spent a lovely day together, a fact witnessed by staff at the Cottage, and then we had sex. Her behaviour just before we had sex was no different to Tessa's. Of course they didn't want to be seen to be willing. In Tessa's case it was probably so she wouldn't be seen as 'easy'.

Perhaps for Rosie it was because she didn't want to be seen to be as 'badly' behaved as Mark. We all know how it works. A bit of faux reluctance at the right time, a bit of "Please stop, Tom," and they don't feel so guilty. It's perhaps not so strange that they used exactly the same phrase when they made their accusations.

I still see Joe Donnelly every once in a while. Not because I particularly want to, but because I feel I have to. I need to keep Joe 'on-side' because he is the only person to whom I have admitted the truth of exactly what happened with Rosie and Tessa. I told him during the course of a very boozy night out in Soho a couple of years ago. In my drunken state, and encouraged by Joe's relentlessly abusive behaviour towards the strippers in a lap-dancing club, I blurted it out. In my confused state, I thought that if anyone would think that Tessa and Rosie got what they deserved, then it would be the woman-hating Joe. I told him that I had completely ignored the fact that both Tessa and Rosie had told me to stop just before I had sex with them.

When I woke up the morning after my night out with Joe, I had a terrible feeling of dread. I couldn't believe that I'd been so stupid. After being so careful, under enormous pressure, for so long, I'd blurted it out for absolutely no good reason. At the time, Joe didn't react at all to what I'd said, but for months I was terrified that he would say something or tell someone else. I decided that if anyone challenged me about it, I would just deny it point blank. As it turned out, no one has ever mentioned my conversation with Joe, not even him. Maybe he was too drunk to remember what I said or perhaps he agreed with me? I don't know and I don't care as long as our conversation doesn't come back to bite me.

My 'version' of what occurred that Sunday night in Rosie's bedroom was formulated before the police even came knocking at my door. I had hoped that maybe Rosie would 'write-off' what happened as a misunderstanding between old friends, but I think I always knew that there were likely to be repercussions. That is why I made sure, before I even arrived home from Butterfield Cottage, that I had my story straight in my head. When I was arrested on my doorstep, I knew exactly what I was going to say to the police. By the time I had told my version of events to Charles, the police and then Jilly, I almost believed it myself.

What did Rosie think would happen when she told Mark? She must have known that there was no way he would deal with, what was essentially a misunderstanding, in a sensible, balanced way. He always had to win, always had to dominate, and this was especially likely bearing in mind his relationship with me. From our first meeting he was intent on proving his superiority. He had to be funnier, more popular, cleverer and better at sport. He always had to win. When we were kids this didn't really bother me, but as we got older – and girls became involved – it did. I could just about cope with the fact that he always had to outperform me on the sports field and in exams, but his drive to be more popular and successful with girls just seemed like rubbing salt into a wound. He always got to choose the best looking girl. When Rosie chose to go bleating to Mark, she had not only made the wrong choice again, she set off a chain of events that would ruin both of them.

Mark probably just assumed that he would be victorious in his latest battle with me. How wrong was he?

# About the Author

Douglas I. Black was born in Bombay and brought up in the UK. He worked in marketing and ran his own business for many years before starting to write. *Get the Girl* is his first novel. Douglas lives in Hampshire with his wife. He has a son who lives in London.

# Acknowledgements

With thanks to Lucy Black, Richard Egan and Caroline Goldsmith

Printed in Great Britain
by Amazon

45040906R00170